JAZZ
& TWELVE O'CLOCK TALES

ALSO BY WANDA COLEMAN

Art in the Court of the Blue Fag (1977)
Mad Dog Black Lady (1979)
Imagoes (1983)
Heavy Daughter Blues: Poems & Stories 1968-1986 (1987)
A War of Eyes and Other Stories (1988)
The Dicksboro Hotel (1989)
African Sleeping Sickness: Stories & Poems (1990)
Hand Dance (1993)
American Sonnets (1994)
Native in a Strange Land: Trials and Tremors (1996)
Bathwater Wine (1998)
Mambo Hips and Make Believe: A Novel (1999)
Love-ins with Nietzsche: A Memoir (2000)
Mercurochrome (2001)
Ostinato Vamps (2003)
Wanda Coleman–Greatest Hits 1966-2003 (2004)
The Riot Inside Me: More Trials & Tremors (2005)
Poems Seismic in Scene, with Jean-Jacques Tachdjian (2006)

Wanda Coleman

JAZZ
&
TWELVE
O'CLOCK
TALES

New Stories

A Black Sparrow Book
David R. Godine · *Publisher · Boston*

This is
A Black Sparrow Book
Published in 2008 by
DAVID R. GODINE · *Publisher*
Post Office Box 450
Jaffrey, New Hampshire 03452
www.blacksparrowbooks.com

Some of the material in this volume is reprinted with the permission of holders
of copyright and publication rights. A list of sources and acknowledgments
begins on page 149.

Book design and composition by Carl W. Scarbrough
The Black Sparrow Books pressmark is by Julian Waters
www. waterslettering.com

LIBRARY OF CONGRESS CATALOGING-IN-PUBLICATION DATA

Coleman, Wanda.
Jazz & twelve o'clock tales : new stories / Wanda Coleman. – 1st ed.
p.   cm.
ISBN-13: 978-1-57423-212-7 (hardcover)
ISBN-10: 1-57423-212-6 (hardcover)
I. Title.   II. Title: Jazz and twelve o'clock tales.
PS3553.O47447J39   2007
813'.54–dc22
2007030237

FIRST EDITION
Printed in the United States of America

For Therese Christensen of Norway
and Audrey Christian of Rodessa—and for Austin

Let us inhale dreamy eternities
From alabaster pipes and sail
Glowing solar boats . . . walk naked
In radiant glacial rains and cool morphic
Thunderstorms . . . shrink into pigmy bo trees
And cast holy shadows on melted cities.

BOB KAUFMAN
from "Solitudes Crowded With Loneliness"

Easing the thing
Into spurts of activity
Before the emptiness of late afternoon
Is a kind of will power
Blaring back its received vision
From a thousand tenement windows
Just before night
Its signal fading

JOHN ASHBERY, "Tarpaulin"

. . . where one relaxes on the axis of the wheel of life . . .

BILLY STRAYHORN, from "Lush Life"

Contents

Joy Ride

SERENE IN THE SIMPLE PLEASURES of afternoon coastal sunshine and the sights beyond their means, the young marrieds, friends since childhood, laugh and joke. They are momentarily above the worries that define their difficult lives. The late-model sedan in which they smoothly cruise is a recent purchase, though not brand new. But happily, they feel as if they are gliding as it takes them through palm-laced residential zones and along wide-laned boulevards, southeast, toward that poorer, darker section of the City of Angels to which they are intangibly restricted.

The radio dial is tuned to a jazz station that renders moods from lively to romantic. The picnic has ended, and thoughts of returning to the world of domestic work and day labor begin to intrude on each individual given temperament.

Husband behind the wheel, the couple up front is married longest, though less than two years, and contemplates children. She's just had the rabbit test, although they're certain of the outcome because of her absent menstrual cycle. The newlyweds in back snuggle in their bliss of mutual exploration. They bubble with the excitement of events and achievements ahead. There is so much they anxiously anticipate accomplishing in that dual future. He'll work during the days and attend school at night. She'll keep working, too, to help build their happy nest.

However, the closer to home they come, the more somber and introspective their thoughts. The merry chatter ebbs. Even the melodic airs become bluesy and discordant, occasionally shrill and punctuated by staccato runs. The harpist, the pianist and the string section defer to brass and woodwinds. The percussionists begin their ascension.

In their palm-dotted neighborhood the streets are narrow, pitted and bumpy, and potholes appear. The car's windows are down, the air warm and clear as sunset nears. Yet the atmosphere inside is oppressive. Newly attempted jokes fall flat. Talk is laconic and rambles, undercut by a generic sadness and the mounting irritability of the driver, who begins to swear under his breath at every traffic gaffe and infraction.

Suddenly, everyone has a gripe about this or that and what about it. Suddenly, it is about time *this* took place and *that* was brought out in the open, and what can decent folk do to *change* whatever-it-is. Suddenly, everyone is edgy and hungry again. Suddenly, everyone is in a hurry to get back to the house, get out of the clothes they've worn all day, kick back and put up their feet. Suddenly, everyone's exhausted.

The newlyweds fall into a doze.

Suddenly, the pregnant wife taps her husband's arm and points. Ahead, there is an object in the middle of the street. A gunny sack. If it is a sack. She thought she saw it move. Please go around it, she asks.

Is she out of her ever-lovin' cotton-pickin' mind?

The tension radiates from his hands, into and out of his mouth. The blast of unearned fury scorches her heart, and she whispers damnation under her breath, remembers the new life she carries, leans into the armrest and closes her eyes. Her withdrawal incites him, and he taps the accelerator. Disturbed by the vibrations, the newlyweds force themselves into alertness, having only half-heard the spat. Over some kind of bag, in the middle of the road?

The radio is broadcasting jassy jazz now, a hot and heavy finger-snapping swing. The rhythm boys are burning under the slide trombone. The newlyweds syncopate as they speculate while the vehicle races forward. A wind-tossed garment. Rags and tatters of some blue heaven. A medicine bag dropped by the local hoodoo man. Love letters from a soldier overseas. Spuds abandoned by some foot-weary shopper. Apples from under an old apple tree. Mittenless kittens nobody has courage to drown.

There's a split-second lull in the music when impact is imminent.

That lull is filled with an infant's spasmodic screams.

The mental sanctuary of their shock is violated as the brass section pours it on and the trumpet player's shrill wail is nearly drowned in the slam of brakes and the shriek of tires. The sedan swerves and stops on a diagonal, coughing out the two men. They trip into the street, which fills with onlookers drawn by the commotion.

The profane sizzle of hot licks issuing from the radio is intrusive. Without a word, a deacon of the old school leans into the car's interior and cuts the sound.

The driver kneels before the bundle. Its burlap fibers ripple slightly, absorbing bodily spill. His hands search the air for the proper grasp. His fingers find a ragged edge and peel it back. There's a tiny chocolate-colored arm perfectly formed. At the end of it sags a miniature doll-like hand with carnation palm and pale pink fingernails. He lowers it, lifts the bundle and stands with the help of his shaken friend. They look at the bundle, are overcome by something nameless, stare to put life back into it.

The two women cry in bewilderment.

Someone says an ambulance is coming. Someone says the authorities have been notified. From blocks around, others come. Adults ring the sedan and shelter its distressed passengers. The children loosely line the curbs, wide-eyed and mute in their peculiar wisdom. The crowd grows larger, swells as the sun wanes, and street lamps lick the early evening sky. The faces of the watchers are all shades of a shared darkness.

In the distant west, a siren wails.

Butterfly Meat

THEY LIVED NOT FAR from the coast. In that summer after-noon's blessed sweet sunshine, the two children followed the heavy-breasted, shapely, sepia woman across the backyard. Blithely, their mother sang nursery rhymes as she marched ahead. The six-year-old loved to help her mother with the laundry. She was eager to impress adults and, therefore, content to carry the basket and clothespin bag. The boy followed but begrudged the chore. Barely five, he frowned as he dragged his basket, under the spell of his father's notions of manhood.

The trio rounded the garage and stopped before a fenceless square chain of land triangulated by three bountiful fruit trees, peach, fig, and lemon. Defined by two hollow iron T-poles, strung with heavy wire lines, the core area was hung with the dazzling rectangular array of the morning's wash flagged briskly by the ocean breeze.

The mother instructed them to study her actions and do their best to do likewise. The children stood against one another, dark spindly arms slack, baskets lowered to knees. They watched as their mother carefully placed her basket in the dried grass before a stiff line of dia-pers clamped end-to-end by clothespins. She stood nearest where the

4

yard ended off an alley, behind her basket, at the extreme end of the line. Then she reached up and tugged the line. Expertly, right hand gliding along, she plucked the pins, gathering as many as one hand could hold before dropping them into the clothespin bag strapped across her shoulder. As she did this, she simultaneously dropped the garments into the basket with her left hand. Feet synchronized to match flying hands, she stepped sideways to the left and tapped the basket with the instep of her right foot, inching it along. Within seconds, she had methodically cleared that line and stood at the end of it, ready to go on to the next.

Appointed two lines each, the children began, working to the music comprised of their mother's rhythmic snatches and humming, the buzzing of flies, and the chirping of birds. Work suddenly turned to fun as they giggled at the underwear, and occasionally dropped a washcloth or hand towel then rushed to shake off any clinging dirt or dried grass. When through, they dashed for the fig tree, scaled it victoriously, and watched their mother below. She soon finished everything except the sheets and called the children down to help fold them.

Giddy with play, the boy and girl ran toward her but were stopped short by the unexpected. Several giant orange monarch butterflies with listless antennae and wings dotted the sheets and blankets, clinging drunkenly as though trapped in the fibers. Fascinated, the children watched.

"Whooooo! Whoosh!"

The mother crept up behind the sheets and shook them.

Startled, the children jumped and screamed as the limp butterflies showered around them to the ground. Amused, the mother admonished them for being silly. Brusquely, she snatched the sheets and blankets from the line and instructed them about the proper way in which to fold the bedding.

Glumly, the children followed their sniggering mother inside, arms aching with the heavy baskets. Dutifully, they set the wash on the dining room table and began to separate items to put them neatly away.

Without warning, the mother's shriek pierced their ears and flipped their stomachs. She held up the sheet in arms that trembled. The children stared at the giant orange butterfly, uncertain. Why was

5

mother screaming? What was there to fear? Yet her hand trembled.

Before they could decipher her apparent terror, their mother ran toward them with a "yoooowwwww," as if she were being devoured by the thing trapped in the sheet. The children turned tail and ran. The mother chased them around the table, the boy in the lead, the girl on his heels. The children cried, snotted, and shouted "Mammmma!," suffering an imagined loss of the mother they loved, devoured by giant butterflies, yet running to keep from being likewise devoured, running as she chased them under the table and through the kitchen. The mother laughed as she yowled.

The children managed to put some distance between themselves and their mother, who prolonged the ordeal by pretending to lose ground. They tiptoed into their bedroom and hid quietly in the closet, behind the door. Above their pounding hearts they could sense their mother's stealth. Suddenly she was at the door trying to get inside. Mother and the giant butterflies eating her alive.

Together, the children clung to the doorknob with all their might, elbows taut, knees bent with the strain, shoes braced to the pine. Their thin brown bodies knocked together in the dark as they struggled to hold the door shut against their mother's powerful pull, their murderous shrieks accompanied by their mother's laughs and taunts, her melodic voice a witch's growl.

"The butterflies are gonna getcha! The butterflies are gonna getcha!"

Pepper

Should've known, if ah didn't know nuthin'. Should've known. . . .
The blues refrain mocked Sandra and her sad confusions spiraled.
She threw her slipper at the radio and collapsed against the table in
tears. The vibrations knocked over her coffee mug. The hot brew ran
to the kitchen floor. Perry's wounded eyes danced in the spill.

They went together "like salt and pepper," everyone cracked. Dark-
skinned Perry loved melon-toned Sandra, but he also loved hanging
out with his homeboys and so, in a symbolic gesture, she wanted to
put salt on his tail.

And that might have been effective had she done so in the wise and
womanly way of the day, and if she had taken into account Perry's being
raised among a southern and superstitious people, his maternal
grandmother in particular (who they said was a two-headed woman).
Whenever he knocked over the saltshaker, he tossed the grains
over his left shoulder. There was a rabbit's foot on every key ring. Once
she found a strange root under her pillow. One washday morning, she
caught his feet in a sweep of the broom. He snatched that broom from

7

her hands and swept the entire apartment. He groaned and yelled whenever she put her purse on the floor. He had a lucky jacket with patches on the sleeve, which he always wore when playing poker. Sometimes, while shopping, when they chanced across an ugly old person, he crossed himself. He had a saint for every occasion, it seemed.

He was always burning this colored candle or that (green to draw money, white for protection). She was choking in the smoke, thinking she was doing her best to tolerate his different background and beliefs. She loved Perry, but his "scary ways" secretly tickled her more and more, sometimes causing laughter, sometimes rankling.

She began to wonder.

In all respects, Perry was the ideal young husband. Her parents were pleased and proud of their new son-in-law. He had good manners and kept himself clean and well dressed. He exercised regularly each morning before going to work. He kept a decent-paying job. He liked sports but enjoyed reading the newspaper at breakfast (noting the astrology column), a novel before bedtime. He was a dancer, up on the latest steps, and there was always a party or two on the weekend. He was a cautious gambler, kept bets small. He gave her every hard-earned nickel except pocket change and expenses. He had given up his church and attended hers. Sandra couldn't imagine a better lover. Then why begrudge him a few hours spent hanging out with his old crowd?

Sandra had a jealous aspect to her nature. She dreaded that one of those late nights Perry might be stolen by another woman. After a couple of her choice complaints, he lightened up awhile. Then, gradually, he resumed activities, giving in to pressures from his friends, most of whom were still single and could not fully appreciate a husband's obligations to his wife. Her misgivings, they declared, were simple silliness. There were no grounds for distrust.

To get her off his back, Perry invited her along one evening. Sandra accepted the challenge, but quickly became bored with the cigarette and cigar smoke, the banter about who had scored what during the big game, and the complex doings of a table sport she could neither play nor was invited to learn. She went out to the car and fumed angrily to music until Perry's night ended and he drove his lovely, seething spouse home.

His tenderness in the night was such that she could not resist him, no matter what had transpired during the day. But in that night's dream-life, she felt scorned, even if that hadn't been the case, and searched sleeplessly for a means of getting even.

The next morning, while Perry showered and dressed, Sandra prepared breakfast, having forgotten her night's intent. But as she set the silverware on the breakfast table, she was seized by an impulse. She picked up the peppershaker, unscrewed the cap, and gently tapped a quarter teaspoon into Perry's black coffee mug.

Within minutes, Perry whisked into the kitchen and planted a smooch on her cheek. He was dressed smartly in shirt and tie, keys with rabbit foot jangling against the change in his pocket when he sat. While he helped himself to the coffee in the percolator, she served plates heaped with eggs-over-easy on grits and hot-water biscuits, then sat down to watch as slyly as she could without giving away her prank.

Perry grabbed the sugar bowl and stirred a teaspoon of raw sugar into the brew. He blew across the steaming mug's surface, took a long, healthy, satisfied slurp and swallowed. Stifling laughter, Sandra filled her mug with coffee and milk, and set the cup to teasing lips, catching his expression as the pepper-spiked coffee went down.

Perry's face purpled and his body went rigid. He stared at her, but his unwavering gaze was uncannily blank. He grabbed his napkin, neatly dabbed his mouth, rose from the table, snatched up his suit jacket, and calmly left the apartment without a word or a glance her way.

Stunned, Sandra sat at the table for hours. Perry did not telephone, nor did he return. She jumped toward the door with every noise. Whenever she heard a car pull to the curb outside, she hurried to the window and, disappointed, stared into the street. Exhausted by the fruitless vigil, she phoned her best friend, LaTonya, who, with her husband's blessing, rushed over, diaper bag and nursling in tow. Second by second, Sandra recounted that morning's events. While the baby slept, they repeatedly examined the incident and the possible offences. None seemed major enough to generate Perry's unexpected reaction. They waited out the night between hot coffee and cold sodas, LaTonya's sincere yet empty reassurances failing to stem the misery and tears. Perhaps, they concluded wearily, it was his way of teaching his bride a lesson.

Sunrise came with the mystery intact.

Weeks passed without news of Perry, either through relatives or friends. If something had happened to him, she was too embarrassed to go to the authorities. He never returned for his belongings. She sent them to him parcel post in care of his grim-lipped parents, followed by weekly tear-filled letters pleading for his return, his love, his understanding. He never answered them, if received. Having lost her means of support, she returned home to confused parents and angry accusations. She couldn't sit down to a meal without reliving that moment. Those early months, her nights without his tenderness were unimaginable punishment. Occasionally, over a steaming cup of coffee at a restaurant or café, she distinctly tasted pepper in the first few sips.

What had she done? What superstitious nonsense did pepper represent?

As the years passed, Sandra returned to school, majored in anthropology, and became an expert in folklore, specializing in the superstitions of Blacks in the southern United States. But she never heard from Perry again. And search as she might, the significance of pepper would elude her forever.

Jazz
at Twelve

WE ARRIVE BEFORE the room fills.

We're decades away from Naptown. We're at Billy D's off the Gold Coast in Malibu. We're dressed in our snazziest. Kevin wears the bronze silk tie I bought him for our first anniversary. We are here for the James Ditzi Quintet, Frank Lattimore on drums. Our main reason for coming is Frank's invitation. Frank and Kevin are running buddies. In his day, not too long ago, Frank was known as one of the greatest stickmen alive. Kevin talks about Frank constantly.

What I don't know is Frank's still shooting up.

We look around. It's a wide space. Roughhewn posts and wood floor-to-ceiling make it cozy, covelike, a ritzy pirates' den. The west wall is all glass and wood columns lined with tiny cocktail tables for two off the main room. I pick one in the middle. Kevin prefers the patio deck outside. There are three tables set for adventuresome listeners, but I seem to chill easily of late and prefer sitting inside. Besides, I'm definitely interested in hearing the music full range.

My name is Babe. I'm Kevin's wife.

They play James Ditzi a lot on KJAS. He's hot for the moment.

I think that's nice, a guy in his late fifties getting that kind of public relations. Especially a White guy. What we Blacks do to The Music leaves scant unexplored. But James has his own signature. Not too many new music guitarists get major radio play. In these days of pop-disco-rock it's tough for jazzniks to draw. They don't teach music appreciation in grade school anymore. A whole generation has grown up without proper ears.

Frank's damned near the same age as James but has had it harder if looks tell. Frank is tall, tan, and lanky with restless arms and elegantly fingered hands. He carries himself like a man who schmoozes for his living. The man was already legend where I grew up. Then one day here he is marching into my living room, trailing Kevin. Stumbling yet. High as in cosmic, his blue-ringed brown irises juiced out at me from under savvy lids. I took one look at him, got instantly evil, and hissed at Kevin.

"Don't bring that scroungy nigger in my house unless he's sober."

This motivated Kevin's tall explaining. That night I find out "the world's greatest drummer" works for the same delivery service Kevin's just hired on with. Kevin is wowed by the man. When he talks his hazel eyes spark as if personally tripping with Frank through every boo joint from Harlem to St. Louie. Kevin promises next time Frank will mind his Ps and Qs. He'll see to it. But in the meantime, Frank did *this*. One time Frank did *that*. Frank went to here-and-there. Frank also played with other greats including bassist Spence Alcohol, and even recorded with "the S.A." on the old Spasmic label. Frank's given Kevin a couple of his mint LPs and a couple of bootlegged vinyls. Sometimes after dinner we fire up and listen. I watch Kevin glow, wishing he could travel backwards in time.

Other reasons I don't like Frank include his cavalier attitude. Like too many musicians of his colored generation he's full of self-hate and self-delusion. It makes him need to indulge his weaknesses—dope and disrespecting women. Plus he's bought the lie that one plays better if one's high. He still conks hair that hasn't had the decency to get gray. And he prefers White women. Blonde if possible. Frank will accept a sistuh when times are hard, but she's got to be fair-skinned. He used to shack with Kevin's mother in the days when she was light enough to pass. Kevin takes after her, but on the olive side, with wavy mink hair slicked back in a foot-long ponytail.

So Frank is the closest thing Kevin's ever had to Daddy.

What I don't know is that in a week or two Spence Alcohol will show up and start to wear the nap off my sofa. He's a honey-skinned bear of a "Black Irishman" who shares Frank's taste in women. He will have just hit the streets, residing at a Hollywood halfway house until his parole officer is placated or until his new lady makes up her mind to marry and support him. He will leave L.A. for Portland in the very near future and will die there before the turn of the century. In the meanwhile, I will make the mistake of thinking Spence is cut out of better rag than Frank. Sometimes I forget the one about birds of like feather. Spence is still strung out also but doesn't shoot it anymore. He smokes it Vietnamese-style.

Our breath is taken by the mauve and gold sunset. Too-blue water laps the shore at our sand-level window. We watch it recede, lulled into its rhythm. Billy D's is a relatively new place on the booming coast.

They're playing vintage Mr. Ellington softly over the PA.

The waiter comes over. I do rapid calculations and figure that by careful nursing we can make Mr. D's mandatory two-drink minimum. Kevin reads me and smirks. He looks at the waiter.

"We're special guests of Frank's."

The waiter gives back the appropriate grimace then takes our orders for a rum and coke duet.

There's noise at the entrance, and James appears followed by his young, black-haired roadie. Lights come on behind Kevin's eyes. One of his not-so-secret ambitions is to be a roadie. Frank's roadie. But Frank's touring days are over, sporadic local gigs his limit. Without a word Kevin goes over to the bandstand, introduces himself, and offers to help set things up. James shakes his hand and accepts. I spy for a beat. Our drinks arrive. I watch the icy dew form on Kevin's glass. I ordered mine without ice. Cold liquids bother me lately, set my teeth on edge.

I don't know I'm pregnant.

Kevin and I are holed up on the upper story of a mid-city four-plex. Our one-bedroom deathtrap rental elicits romantic nods of approval

13

from friends and dread from my parents. It's a funky vermin-ridden cavern owned by a merciless survivor of Treblinka. On the first day of every month I curse the Nazis for having bled the humanity out of her. She insists on cash payment and I insist on receipts. When I put the money in her talons, my eyes are invariably drawn to the sea-gray numbers swimming in liver spots, blood warts, moles, assorted scars, and blotches.

I work the ten-key punch from nine-to-five for a medical supply outfit. My wage-slave pay barely keeps us in rent, utilities, and food when Kevin doesn't work. When he does we manage to have a few extras, go out more, dream a little. Of course I see to all the duns. I'm not stingy, just cautious. It's always a bitch on the meatless end of the bone. I worry as I scrimp. But even when things are tight, I make a special effort to budget Kevin pocket money. He'd rather make his own, does when he can, but there are economic limits on unskilled high school grads. At least I've got office and accounting skills. Since we've been together, Kevin's rarely kept a job longer than three or four months.

What I don't know is that my rare coin collection will turn up missing in a couple of months. It will be followed by a disappearance of the cash I had hidden in a sealed envelope behind the oranging Modigliani print over the living room couch.

I don't crab about Kevin's smoking habits. He's made several attempts to turn me on, but I seem to have some strange immunity. He's quit trying to educate me into it and either smokes alone or with the guys. Even so, I have no objections to living a little bit outside the Law, just enough to mute survival pressures.

Once in a while Kevin comes up with a kilo of sans. He breaks down the brick of weed, cleans it, and bags it into lids. He keeps a couple of ounces for his personal stash then barters the rest. We burn the cash on clothes, auto repairs, and other needs. One time he bought himself a very used electric bass guitar. The last time he bought me an eighteen-carat gold slave bracelet. A year from now I will pawn it at less than a quarter of its worth to buy antibiotics for the baby.

The sun has set into the Pacific. The room is slightly cooler and the waitress is lighting the little red candle lamps that sit in the midst of each table. This is the way to groove, I think, in no rush, unconcerned. One thought meandering after another. I watch Kevin clown with James on the bandstand. He admires the electric guitars and mandolin. James laughs as Kevin bows his legs and pretends to strum the mandolin, his eyes skyward, doing his Hendrix imitation. Kevin would sell his soul for the ability to play. But all he can do is admire the talent of others. He's a freak for most kinds of music and likes all of it loud. We have quite a sound system at home, one of those quadrasonic models that makes sound travel around the room, speaker to speaker.

Kevin hates it when I'm cynical about the music business. The chilly fickle industry, which has marginalized me, fails to stem his childlike worship. "Music is my religion," he told me one night as we made love to Pink Floyd.

What I don't know is Kevin's got another habit. He hides his outfit behind the old forty-fives I never play anymore in the bottom of the record cabinet. During a snit of spring fever I will find the cotton balls, the test tube, the syringe, and the rubber hose.

When Kevin comes in nights he's fairly wired. He likes running the streets so a job making deliveries suits him. He prides himself on having learned every shortcut in Los Angeles. The company he works for is so ramshackle benefits are minimal. There's no accident or medical insurance coverage and don't even dare think dental. Kevin drives a funked-up little black Dodge Dart. He's put a citizens band radio in it and spruced it up with mud flaps, a new set of fat gangster whitewalls and chrome-spoked rims. He plans to have the windows tinted. There's a black and yellow bumper sticker that reads, "Mafia Staff Car."

What we don't know is that three weeks from now we will go to the Pandemonium to see a play by Mtui Sambusa, the Black feminist poet. It's another culturally correct event we'll sacrifice to see at my insistence. I will cry in my seat. Kevin will comfort me. When we exit to the theatre parking lot we will find the window of his Dart smashed. The CB will be ripped out of the dash and the tires will be missing—rims and all. Kevin will talk the parking lot attendant into letting us leave the car there overnight. Spence Alcohol will drive

Kevin to the junkyard the next morning for rusted replacement rims and retreads.

I sit at an angle facing the bandstand. I look up and see James Ditzi trailing Kevin to our table. In a funny way, Kevin likes to brag about having me as his wife. I moonlight as a songwriter. Ten years ago I lucked into a musician's workshop and became the hit of their Tuesday night showcase. One of my songs was picked up by a major rhythm-and-blues star who was scouting incognito. Within the year my opus bulleted up the charts and went semi-solid gold. I made a nice piece of coin on the publishing—enough for two years without having to "sweat the man." I thought my career was made. I didn't know about one-hit wonders.

James has heard my name around, he says. He's even had three or four occasions to play jazz renditions of my song "Too Too Bad For Me." I smile appropriately ladylike and thank him. He's scared I'm going to reach into my tote and abracadabra lead sheets. But I keep my hands nested around my drink. He relaxes when he sees he's not being hustled. There's a big half laugh, half bark across the room and we look up to see Mr. Spence making his way towards us. He and James Ditzi go all the way back to a one-night stand in Jersey. Kevin makes sure I'm introduced. Spence has heard of me also.

We exchange a bit of loose industry chitchat. Then James goes out back to talk money. Spence goes with him to meet Mr. Billy D who's enclaved in his very private office. I've heard Mr. D doesn't mingle with us nobodies.

What we don't know is that the weather will be unusual this winter. There will be volcanic action in Hawaii and monsoon-like swells off the coast of Southern California. A few wealthy seaside dwellers will lose their dream homes. A couple of cliffside mansions will be splashed onto Pacific Coast Highway by heavy rainfall. Several sturdy piers will be washed away. Billy D's will be flooded, and by Christmas its doors will forever shut.

The rest of the combo shows. Piano is Jefty Lerner, swift, small-boned, and smart in Ben Franks and a three-piece suit. All the men are suited. But Jefty looks like he should be teaching high school English somewhere. Then Robin Roy shows, the very tall, very bulky, cask-chested reedman who reddens when he blows. He looks like James Ditzi's younger, stouter brother. He favors dark solid colors while James is vested under fine pinstripes and a crisp white dress shirt with studs. There's Clark Wiggins, a horn man obviously under the influence of Miles Davis. They begin tuning up and the evening's patrons gradually spill into the room.

Kevin's out of things to do and sits across from me with a mild case of jitters, eager to see Frank. He's started firing cigarettes, one after the other. Every few seconds he turns and scans the room, exit to exit. Early is a word foreign to Frank's vocabulary. The only time he's prompt is when it's time to score.

Becky, Frank's "main squeeze," he likes to call her, shows up. She's a slight but sturdy, freckle-skinned blonde young enough to be Kevin's half sister. She's riding with her even younger brother. They have to flash IDs before security allows them to sit. She waves at James, then spots Kevin and comes over to our table to say hello. We've met before and I'm always friendly; nevertheless, she's acutely aware of my prejudice though no one else seems to notice. She's a dispatcher for the same delivery company employing Frank and Kevin. After pleasantries, Becky steers her brother to a front table near where the drums will sit.

What she doesn't know is that three days from now she'll place a frantic call to Kevin, out of her skull because Frank's been arrested for beating her. Neighbors will have complained and the police will be only too willing to oblige, especially after making note of Frank's new tracks. She's so much in love she will refuse to press charges but they'll hold him on an old drug beef. What I don't know is that I'll be feeling generous enough to reach deep into my emergency stash for Frank's bail.

A pretty, brown-skinned woman about my age goes up to James and they rap a bit. She's a singer copping the chops of the Fancy Miss Nancy from frosted fried hairdo to choreographed hand movements. She even mimics that cool, frozen Las Vegas smile. I pray she won't sing "All In Love Is Fair." I'm still in my late Billie Holiday phase although I'm starting to look more like a slightly pudgy Lena Horne.

Kevin jumps to his feet and rushes across the room. Frank has just come in, lugging one of his drums. He's wearing white work gloves to protect his hands. I wonder how he manages to get all his equipment into that tore-up old Volks. I watch as he lowers the drum, pockets the gloves, and exchanges hand slaps with Kevin. Then I watch as Kevin hoists the drum into its place on the bandstand while Frank watches, smiling.

Becky scurries over and gives Frank a big rub-a-dub hug. He kisses her on the nose then pats her rear as she scoots back to her table. Spence joins them and the room momentarily fills with staccatos of laughter. The S.A. points to the bar where he'll anchor for the evening. Then Kevin and Frank go back outside to finish unloading.

I take out the little leatherette notebook I always carry in my tote. Should a few notes start to kick around inside my head I like to be ready. Or should the opening words of a lyric—or even a refrain—find their way to my mind's ear. I keep my little books of songs ritualistically. I date them and make notes as to when and where they're composed. I'm living for the day when women's music will receive as much attention as men's or dying for the day of my posthumous discovery by some lover of innovative fusion. In the interim, dolor in lieu of fame does. Taking the bus to and from the job does. Relying on someone else to pick up the tab on nights like this does. Living on the edge of Kevin's fear does.

Tune-up ends and serious business begins. Instantly the room is transformed. This could be the Five Spot. This could be Birdland. This could be a maiden voyage on a spaced-out ship into the inner regions of night. Kevin is sitting across from me now. He's giving me his moonful look, the one that tells me I'm beautiful. Whenever he does, I suddenly hear Nat King Cole singing "Angel Eyes."

I feel the words of a lyric forming. Kevin watches, thoughtfully smoking a cigarette as I write. I know there's a joint in the glove compartment for the drive home. I glance oceanward time to time and refresh my inspiration in the window light dancing on the tide. The words flow as smoothly as the opening number "Eleanor Rigby."

James dominates the set then gives each artist a little taste. Frank is the essence of mellow and evokes a couple of throaty enthusiastic "yeahs," one of them Kevin's.

18

The guest, "Miss Fancy" lady vocalist, rises, steps to the bandstand and after a brief introduction, eases her way to the mike. Very sweetly, James chords the opening of "My Funny Valentine." She's not bad at all and, after a significant career move, will someday be a major league contralto. I go fluttery inside and fall into Kevin's orbs as she wrings out my heart.

What I don't know is that soon after the baby arrives Kevin will take his clothes and split.

The third piece is a rephrasing of Wes Montgomery's "Bumpin'" with phenomenally lighter, tighter, yet more complex fingering by James. However, all ears are on Frank Lattimore.

The man on drums steals the attention effortlessly. I see why he doesn't work regularly, besides the dope which, in this business, never seems to keep anyone of the Bright Persuasion from earning *mucho dinero*. Especially after they confess and repent. Part of Frank's problem is that he isn't repentant enough. The rest is the man's bloody genius. In this town, anything even hinting of excellence is immediately put on ice. Especially if it's one of Us. Frank is the only Negroid on the bandstand.

By the fourth number, "You Are My Sunshine," James decides not to fight it. Frank dominates the ensemble yet gives it back a more cohesive self. He's not greedy and James obviously appreciates this. But I don't really hear James anymore, meaning the guitar specifically. I'm lost in the combined sounds. Totally. Frank has tranced the entire room.

During intermission Frank will be approached by a wealthy young man from Japan. He will offer Frank grand theft dough for private lessons—more scratch than Frank's seen in his entire career. Frank will thank him and say no.

This is not a man playing drums. This is a man caressing a woman. The only woman he's true to. She's as Black as the Congo, as wide as the Atlantic, as glorious and as illusive as heaven promised here and now. She is as water rises to tongue the troubled shore with shimmers of foam. She is the heady pungency of fresh after-sex. She is the desolation of being a gifted, recalcitrant stranger in one's native land.

Amen.

What Frank doesn't know is that there's another young woman taking notes that night. She's a reporter for the *Times*. She is pale, ashen blonde, and of lofty attitude. She will pen a rave review tonight. It'll run tomorrow. It will praise every member in the Ditzi group . . . except Frank. He will be mentioned fleetingly as being "on drums." I will read it aloud to Kevin and he will snot up with rage and kick over one of the stereo speakers.

But right now, tonight, my head is bursting as another lyric finds me. I stab my little notebook in swift, ecstatic jabs, caught in the thrall. Now Frank's on the brush, devilishly whisking the skins. Now he kisses the cymbal ever so blithely.

Kevin can't take his eyes off his step-dad. I'm almost amazed into excusing Frank's earthly transgressions. If I weren't so uptight I'd thank him for reminding me why I love music and the witchery of transforming pain into exquisite loveliness.

Kevin and I share weepy little smiles as the set breaks. We lean into our tiny table and start hungrily frenching as the waiter brings our second round of drinks.

What we don't know is that on the first day of winter, Frank's old VW will be spotted apparently abandoned on a convenience store parking lot after curfew. The great Mr. Lattimore will be found late of an overdose of what most folks will prefer to call heroin. It will be one of those exceptionally bright, smogless, cloud-flecked days we have in this region. I'll stand on the veranda looking out towards the hills of Silver Lake. The baby will be sleeping quietly out back. I'll be listening to one of the old Spence Alcohol cuts featuring Frank Lattimore on drums, grateful Kevin left the music behind.

Winona's Choice

"We were bone deep. Know the saying?"

"Yes. I know what you mean. It's like that, sometimes."

"It made keeping our vows easy. Cuz I thought I wasn't the marryin' kind. But, I felt complete whenever I was in her arms. And time didn't change it, if it changed us. It made it deeper."

"I envy you. We never had a chance to experience that—my man and I. But I can imagine."

WHEN THE CLOCK'S ALARM went off at the wrong time, it caught Maureen's stare climbing the gray quake-instigated cracks along the walls and on the ceiling. Patiently, she reset the alarm and wound the clock. A persistent yearning had tortured her into fitfulness. She needed more sleep but could not force her eyes shut. The telephone rang. She scooped up the heavy black receiver, yawning loudly enough for the caller to hear.

"Hey Reeny-Reeny, wake up. The sun is shining."

'Twas Julian. La-dee-da. One of those low-down-dirty pangs went shamooom. All she had to do was see him on television for the first time in four years and within hours her phone rang—Julian coochie-

coochie on the other end of her line—like psychic it seemed. They had gone together a year off and on. Talk about the bad penny turning up, Julian was more like a bad half-dollar.

"Uh—hello, Julian." She stopped herself from calling him by her old love name for him, Ju-Jee. He had killed that innocent part of her affection with his crude exit. Now she was uncertain what to call him. Jules when she felt close, Julian when she felt edgy, distant or angry.

"You sleep?"

"Just about."

"Been faithful, Maureen?"

"No. I haven't."

"Lover dear, you really hurt my feelings when you went and married that dude."

"Did I?"

"You two still together?"

"No."

"I figured."

Julian had his blue nerve, nutting-off behind her hard fortune. Especially when he knew nothing about her everything.

"Losing her was terribly hard. All the platitudes and sympathetic silences didn't mean a damn. I went straight to the bottom. Alcohol and any dope I could find. I wanted to join her in death. But something wouldn't let me."

"She wouldn't let you."

"Hey—I bet you're right. She always wanted the best for me, and always refused to let me indulge my weaknesses. She kept building me up, no matter how much the world tore me down."

"You were lucky to have those years together. My husband was taken before we even had a chance. Our time together was so short, I have to look at his picture sometimes to remember his smile. I feel so cheated."

Russell "Rusty" Eberhart and Maureen Jayne Dix had met at her distant cousin's wedding. He was the friend of a friend of the groom's, seeking a bride of his own. She was a single clerical worker hoping to better her station in life. Their romance was swift and intense. She said yes. Their ceremony was held in the minister's chamber two weeks later. Rusty gave up his place for hers. She kept her job at Quadravista. During the day he sold clunkers on a renegade uncle's used automobile lot. His liquor store night job was "the honest gig," he loved to joke, taken to earn extra pennies down on their dreams of a home and children.

One Sunday, Maureen was awakened before dawn by a knocking so urgent the memory still made her stomach roil.

Police officers were at the door.

Tragedy had made its rounds that Saturday night, shortly before curfew. A ski-masked bandit had entered the liquor store where Rusty manned the register alone and unarmed. Unawares, a young couple interrupted the robbery-in-progress. Rusty shouted a warning. Foiled, the enraged shooter had fired into Rusty's chest then fled. The maximum efforts of paramedics had proved useless. The police scenario had cast Rusty as the hero. However, in the hellish aftermath, Maureen had found little beyond irony in so supreme a sacrifice paid in the name of minimum wage earned at maximum drudge.

The robber-murderer was never apprehended.

Maureen was adrift in the days after.

Russell Eberhart received a posthumous commendation from city officials and an insurance settlement shared with the Eberharts. Rusty's family, good people who were strangers, disappeared from her sphere within weeks of the funeral. She was given time off the job but returned early to keep involved. Those terrible nights she cried herself to sleep. Eventually, she donated most of his belongings, his sports equipment, and clothes to a church charity. She traded in his Jeep and her sedan on a third automobile and paid it off with what was left of the insurance money. Their wedding pictures, his wedding band, and other keepsakes were stored in an old traveler's chest.

"I felt rage and confusion. I raged at the hospital, the doctors, but mainly at God for taking her. I wanted to be taken too. Wherever she was . . . whatever heaven, hell . . ."

"I missed him. And I was confused. I was angry at his killer. In addition, at the liquor store owners. Even that couple he'd sacrificed himself for. They still had each other. But what did I have?"

* * *

Two years crept past. Yet the wound was tender.

She lived in that thin space between a classless Black ghetto population and the streets, spent the evenings taking self-improvement courses at a community college, a halfhearted pursuit of something in which to invest her passions. Dates were rare, her interest in men fleeting. Until Julian disturbed her solitude, Maureen had not given sex much thought.

In that brief past, whenever Julian appeared before them on television, she had enjoyed pointing him out to Rusty, cracking jokes or sneering.

"*That* drove me straight into your arms!"

"Be polite and thank the man, Babe!" Rusty would tease, confident.

Strangely, the last time she had heard from Julian was on their wedding night. They had consummated coupling and were wrapped arms-and-eyes, bodies dripping sweat and sweetness, when the phone rang.

"Damn!" They parted reluctantly, Rusty reaching it by its third ring. "Yeah? Huh?" His eyes danced with amusement as he climbed back into bed, tugging the cord, clamping the mouthpiece. "All yours, Maureen—one of your old beaus—mad as a wet hen, horny as a toad."

They stifled snickers as she took the receiver. Rusty pulled Maureen snug against his dark, muscular nakedness as she positioned the receiver between his ear and hers.

"Yes?"

"Reeny, it's me, Julian. I'm in town."

"Long time no hear."

"'Zat your boyfriend?"

"Husband. We're fresh-married."

There was an intake of breath and a pause. "That shouldn't make any difference between us."

Rusty convulsed, holding his laughter.

"It does-for me. He's about my age too."

"Oh. You're in *love* and all that twaddle."

"Yes, very much so."

"Then I guess there's nothing to talk about."

"Guess not."

The receiver was slammed angrily in their ears. They laughed until their sides ached. Afterwards, they made love again then shared a long silence in the dark.

"That guy, who called. What'd you say his name is?"

"Julian Stoat."

"Yeah. Well, he may be a big-shot movie actor, Maureen—but he ain't nuthin' but a clown in my book, passin' up a dream-come-true like you, Babe."

The call had been forgotten but recollection stirred Maureen inexplicably. Why hadn't she told Julian she had been widowed?

"So tell me, Reeny, what happened to y'all."

"*Us* all is none of your business, Julian."

She was loath to admit to herself what she suspected he truly thought of her, but knew she would rather live with his misperceptions than allow him to soil the beauty of her tragically brief marriage.

"Suits me. I thought you might like to boohoo on my shoulder."

"Thanks, no thanks."

"Good girl! Takin' it like a man. I've always dug that about you, Reeny. Yes, sir—it's me and you. Now, give me that address again and I'll pick you up tomorrow for brunch, soon as my plane lands."

"I'm still workin' the phones at Quadravista in Culver." She cringed at having to say this, realizing it was tantamount to confessing that she had not progressed much beyond the grip of poverty and that she was needy in more ways than one.

"No sweat. Lunch'll do. How much time can you steal?"

"She was your complexion, very dark, tall, lovely. Breasts just right—enough for the palms to cup but not cover. That's why he brought you here. Squinting in this light . . . I could swear . . ."

"That's what he meant when he told me about Winona."

"Is this a setup?"

"Yes. He wants me to fuck you and then tell him who's the better lover."

"You're a beautiful woman. I'd like to fuck you."

* * *

Theirs had been at-odds gravity. He was the oldest man she had ever dated. She had never been quite certain what that attraction was, either way, particularly his heart to hers. She had found the roguish actor an exciting change from the kind of "nice" men she usually sought yet found so rare. Julian's self-possessed maturity reduced most of Maureen's guy peers to adolescence; yet he also had his childlike aspects, spontaneity and a greed for attention. He also had style. He was the jazzy type she had always fantasized about—half Count Basie, half James Brown—an aficionado of things feminine, generous as long as she asked for nothing.

Whatever Mr. Stoat wanted from women, Mr. Stoat usually got as one of Hollywood's few long-working veteran actors of African-American descent. He had paid his share of dues and did not feel obligated to play for keeps or to uplift the downtrodden. He had made a spanking new career move, and was pulling down grand theft dough as the articulate wisdom-cracking Negro sidekick in *Reno and The Night Fighter*, a primetime television cop opera. As far as Maureen knew, he had several other women, supported two ex-wives but no children, and preferred living in the Bay Area, commuting to and from Los Angeles by plane.

"My low-toned Daddy introduced me to *pulchritude*, clap and crab lice in a St. Louis bawdy house when I was twelve." He hadn't survived six decades only to "die of utter fright in some tramp's bed," as he had put it, and had sampled amply of scandal "behind my behind." Black-mail, extortion, alimony—"I've been all those nasty places and have done all of that," he had warned. When Julian Stoat flew into "The Wood," he didn't have time to cruise. He was afraid of "those skanky bitches on The Boulevard," as he put it, more afraid of "heat stroke," that is, of being arrested as a john by the police.

He had been put in more than enough high-priced tricks. The mature Julian wanted an "undercover lover" who would avail herself to him whenever he deemed it necessary, whatever the circumstance —an independent "healthy" woman who would tend her backyard scrub and keep out of his private Eden. Despite a monogamous streak miles wide, Maureen seemed trimmed to order. Yet she resented the way in which Julian kept tabs on her via telephone. His calls always came late at night, calculated, she knew, to catch her in bed. She felt entitled to other lovers—*if she wanted them*. She had not. Yet, now her heart squirmed in its starvation for anything that vaguely approximated the gratifying companionship she had enjoyed with Russell. While he was not generous on that account, her body could not deny Julian his lingering impression. She had fallen for him once. His was the power to resurrect the love he had once destroyed. Fate, Julian surmised, ruled in his favor, since Maureen had known him longer than Rusty and as intensely.

"Meet me Reeny? I know it's been a shamefully long time."

"When and where, Jules?"

"You used to call me Ju-Jee. My flight gets into LAX around midnight. They've got me a limousine replete with chauffeur and champagne on ice. They're putting me up at the Plateau. But, uh, look, Lover —hang on a second . . ."

"Is he really drunk out there, or pretending?"

"I don't know. He really is a terribly good actor."

"Then let's play him for all it's worth."

"I don't mind that at all."

"Actually, I enjoy talking to you. I haven't had anyone to talk to in years. Never about Winona. Never my deepest feelings."

"It's like that with me too. I'm too young to be a widow, I keep saying. But I don't know how to come back from it. I don't know who to talk to about Rusty."

While she listened to his rustlings around, she wondered how she had let herself get hung up over a man thirty-plus years her senior. Especially an olive-toned coot who had made it resoundingly clear that the only thing he ever intended to settle into was a crypt. Memory kicked in and kicked up.

Four years ago, it had been charm at first sight. They had passed one another several times in the hallways at Quadravista, a cinema production outfit. Each time she had felt his eyes under her skirt. Julian was costarring in the remake of a film based on a Chester Himes novel. He had been cast as the savage academic intellectual who takes

27

on Ed Coffin in the streets of Harlem for a fortune in contraband. One of the secretaries had been ill during negotiations, and the boss-lady asked Maureen to step in and take fast notes. That evening, as she thumbed up his rakish history from the yellowing back pages of her *Spade* magazine collection, the phone rang. He had taken up temporary residence in the city until the film finished shooting. He was lonely. She accepted his invitation for spumante and scrambled eggs the next morning. He showed up outside her door in a tore-down convertible, toting a blender in need of repair.

"Hang with me, Reeny, 'til I drop this thing off."

He hopped out and left her with the motor running and the radio blasting rhythm and blues. On his return to the appliance store parking lot, he jumped her from her lips down, kissing and smacking. Her efforts to return the favor, while he wheeled through traffic, caused him to nearly rear-end a city bus. They laughed themselves sore behind a flurry of curses and honks. The world was fun whenever they got together.

He telephoned once or twice a day and saw her four or five times a week, asking her to stay the nights. Yet, he kept a distinct, if indefinable distance. He was always out of reach on holidays, never called to wish her a happy anything, and never sent cards or gifts. Experience had armed him with a dicey elusiveness the twenty-six-year-old stubbornly believed she could either match or overcome. But as the weeks passed, Maureen realized she could do neither.

During the final days of his shooting schedule, Julian was coy to the point of oiliness. The film he'd been hired for would soon close production and it would be time to return home. Maureen had fallen in love with his acrimonious self and he knew it. But he did not invite her to join him. On the day she decided she cared enough to accept him on his stingy terms, he dropped her off outside her apartment complex and sped off in that tore-down convertible coupe without a promise or a goodbye. She had expected to hear from him the next day. When she called his hotel, she discovered he had checked out. Now he dared pick up with her four years later as if nothing had happened.

Why was she allowing him the liberty?

"Ready, Reeny—that address again."

"You sure, Julian?"

"When I get finished lickin' you head to foot, you'll forget we were ever apart."

"For days I wallowed in self pity. I neglected myself. I left my saxophone in its case and quit practicing. Things got so bad, I had to hock it. Friends offered me jobs and loaned me money to help me keep going. I don't know how I made it. I didn't see people unless I had to. I sat here in the dark, listening to old records on that turntable in there. Sometimes I'd play along—if I were out of hock. Smoke up a storm. Drink myself stupid. Get high. Wake up. In the streets—sometimes a strange woman's bed. Rolled. Beat up. Didn't care who I was or where. . . ."

"I slept a lot. Like I wanted to sleep forever. I don't have your habits. But I didn't eat. And if I hadn't kept working, I probably would've starved myself to death, if I didn't drown myself in the bathtub first. . . ."

Julian's call had left her restless. She forced herself to read and watch television, but nothing registered through her heat. She was in for a wait until his plane touched down. Then what? A cold shower actually helped defuse her anxiousness.

When she climbed into bed, she clicked on the clock radio. An old Delphonics tune doo-wopped Maureen into a nearly forgotten state of soulfulness. It had been one of Rusty's favorites.

"Hot damn, Reeny! You look like money!"

It was another typical Julian broadcast staged to draw everyone within range. He had directed the limo driver to park directly in the building's entrance. He had managed to sign a couple of autographs before being directed to her floor by security. It took a half-hour before her coworkers, and her supervisor, had finished gushing over the striking, if not tall, Mr. Stoat. He had decked himself out in a tan silk shirt and maroon designer suit and was radiant from the top of his shaved-smooth dome to the tips of his Italian suede loafers. A slight paunch exaggerated his dignified pose but my-my he didn't look a day over forty-sumpthin' off camera. Maureen thought him every pound the giant chocolate koala, cute but dangerous. He charmed her boss-lady into giving Maureen the rest of the day off. Thus, to the envious eyes of coworkers, he whisked her from her desk straight to the Plateau's penthouse suite.

The kissy digs were spectacular, art deco revisited, high ceilings and archways, Egyptian love seats and divans, shaped tinted mirrors, lamps as elegant as date palms, a sunken lavishness one stepped down into upon entry. From the proper angle, all of downtown could be viewed, glowing gold in temperate afternoon sun. She was overcome by the surroundings and swooned. Startled, he gripped her arms and half carried her to one of the divans. She was embarrassed. He was oddly sympathetic.

"Too rich for you. I know the feeling, Reeny." He smiled but didn't impart the memory. "Wait here. I'll get us a drink."

She closed her eyes to collect herself. On his way to the kitchenette, he hit a button and the room filled with coolly erotic orchestrations. The mood, the music, and trail of his spicy aftershave revived one of their languid meetings on the low-rent end of Hollywood. It had been the only time Julian had broached a serious subject.

"I bet you used to be religious, Reeny."

"Not particularly. I was raised in the church. Like most, I guess."

"Baptist. I betcha."

"Like most. But as they say—in this town, the dollar is all the God you need."

He had liked that. "For a ghetto child, you've got brains. Indeed."

Whatever his childhood worship, he had abandoned it. Without fail, Julian rose before each sunrise for Zen meditation. She would read in bed. He also practiced a type of Japanese swordplay and had given her a demonstration that same afternoon. Afterwards, he took a ritualistic bath, came to her naked beneath his black kimono, read her haiku aloud for foreplay, and displayed a silver snuffbox of cocaine.

"High-octane blow, Reeny. I'll never destroy myself with any of that cheap street shit." He had opened the robe and revealed his erection. She had followed his finger to her knees. "Take it and sprinkle it right there."

She had begun to do as commanded.

"Nowww—lick it all off, *Winona*."

30

"Wha?" Groggily she had stopped and raised her head.

"Lick it all off, Reeeny, *deeearessst.*"

She had wondered vaguely about this slip at the time but had dismissed it, preoccupied with the task of his pleasure-and all of that before breakfast. She did not like oral sex and he knew it. Afterwards, she washed out her mouth with red wine, drank half the bottle before she stepped into a hot shower and scalded their day from her flesh, all the while chiding her weakness. If he could appreciate the refinements of another culture, what was his problem with her in their culture? Or was it simply that he was still in love with a dead woman? It was difficult not to feel competitive to this Winona, whoever she had been.

Now her elusive lover had returned. Pretensions aside, Julian was crude and delighted in trashing her romantic notions—as great a frustration as fascination. What was in store for her in this new go-round?

"If you don't mind undressing for me, I'd like to look at your body while we talk."

"No, I don't mind at all."

"Do it slowly. Start with the outer garments. And take off those spangles. Let me clothe your natural sensuality with my eyes. . . ."

He made a noise and she opened her eyes. They were back in the Plateau's penthouse suite. He had returned in a gray velvet smoking jacket with an uncorked bottle of champagne and crystal tube glasses.

"Reeny—I've ordered us a fabulous lunch. We'll light up a joint, eat, then you'll help me memorize that script over there." The coffee table was a sleek oval of iced glass and brass, a thin manuscript to one edge. "Then, maybe, we'll think about doin' that other thang later."

"Toast?"

"You say it, Julian."

"To lovers who are *friends.*"

She failed to appreciate the emphasis. "Sounds like a book title."

The champagne was chilly—blond and pleasingly dry.

"Think of me as—the Author. Like that?" His eyes sparked with boyish mischief. He smiled as he set his emptied tube by the sheaf of papers. With a hardy bounce, he threw himself on the divan. Maureen was intrigued. He fired the joint of marijuana and studied her as she studied him between sips and tokes.

"You lookin' mighty impish, Jules."

Her observation pleased him. "Reeny, you don't know what you've got." He smacked his thick Mandarin lips.

"Huh?"

"You're quite a dish. Statuesque, poised . . . and," he licked his fat violet tongue at her, ". . . tempestuous. When a man looks at you, he wants to bring you down scale, to exalt in his conquest."

"Jesus, Julian." She colored.

"No jive." He leaned back, eyes traveling her high bodice, jean-hugged curves, sandals on shapely feet, healthy pink nails. "And, best of all, you're genuine. No artifice. No makeup, nothing fake. Even that Afro bush you're still wearing–kinky and ebony. You're the personification of clean, unadulterated excitement."

What, she wondered, had brought this bull into the barn?

"I mean it. Seriously."

Room service provided black china and real silver against rose damask. There were oodles of blanched and sliced Spanish onion, olives, walnuts, and feta cheese on a bed of assorted tender greens with a bowl of spicy vinaigrette salad dressing. A half-dozen pats of sweet butter graced a plate piled with the most varied assemblage of warm rolls she had ever seen or tasted. Dessert could be plucked from a bowl–effusion of fresh-washed peaches, muscat, concord and red grapes, and applepears. Julian, she remembered, was a vegetarian.

"'S this okay, Reeny? I forgot. You still eat meat."

"Veggie's fine with me as long as it's not pasteboard and dandelions."

"You're a beauty. In my younger days, I would have fought him for your favors and won."

"I bet you would've."

"My daddy was well-heeled and a White man. Of all the guys in our crowd, Julian's the only one who's never stopped holding it against me. As tight as we've been, boys roughin' and toughin' together–all of that, from sharing the same woman to covering each other's back in a scrape . . . and

*there's still this thing between us. My lightness, his darkness. He's always
envied me my secret, no matter that I've told him a hundred times I don't have
a secret. The physical has little to do with it. What money I had was wasted
long ago. Position doesn't even merit discussion. Women like me because of
the way I treat 'em."*

*"I'm always amazed when jes bein' in the company of a man is as good as
sex itself. That's happened to me. Quiet time can be like that. When a man
and a woman touch in a place that—like you said—it's deeper than the skin's
surface or its color."*

"May I kiss you?"

"Of course."

She was enchanted. They enjoyed their meal in a profoundly satisfy-
ing and thoughtful silence through which the mellow jazz coursed.
He made goo-goo eyes at her, occasionally waving his forefingers
giddily to the rhythms, playing the cosmic conductor. When she finished, she set her plate aside, went to the window, and looked out on
the vista beyond.

"Time for work, Reeny." He clapped his hands to break her reverie.

She spun around and raised an eyebrow. "Work?"

"My script. Remember?" He teased his uppers with his tongue. "It's
only a couple of pages. Here—a copy for you, a copy for me. I memo-
rized most of it on the plane down. It's moronically simple."

She puzzled over it. "A commercial!"

"For dog food, yet. There're several versions of the same thing, in
case. They're paying mighty big bucks. Not to mention residuals. C'mon
and help me with this. They're taping between five and eight tonight.
I'll drop you at your crib on the way. Then, maybe, we'll rendezvous
afterwards."

"Cool."

"Okay. Now, I'll say it the way I remember it. You correct me when
I'm wrong."

"Gotcha."

"Hey, has your Champ got that hangdog feeling? Remember, folks.
Your pooch—"

"Wait, wait. It's 'Hey folks,' and 'Remember, your pup—.'"

33

He repeated it, then—"needs multivitamins. To be sure he gets all the nourishment he needs. Just like we humans."

"Drop the 'we.'"

"Just like humans. For a glossy coat, good strong teeth and healthy bounce—that hangdog feeling!"

"Uh—that goes 'strong healthy teeth' and 'hound dog,' steada sayin' 'hang' again."

In minutes he had it down, complete with characterization and pose. His transformation of patent silliness into entertainment delighted her. He even wagged his own boxy tail to boot, in a dignified-sissy manner. She spilled over with laughter. He reached for her and began stroking her between kisses. She reclined and he straddled her. There was no time for napping afterwards. He roused her, they dressed and relaxed over coffee he made fresh in the kitchenette.

"Don't knock these commercials, Reeny. They may seem trivial in the span of a true actor's career, but you can't beat the exposure."

"I know you don't want to hear this, but I admired you when I was a kid. Everything you did was always excellent, considering-"

"But! You wished my parts were meatier, the scripts better written, and would've preferred my characters a little less clownish."

She purpled.

"Look—the Man don't care who we are. Acting's a job. Like being a receptionist. You take what you can get and you do your best at it. That's why I've survived, why I've kept working when a hundred others have fallen by the wayside. I lick no ass but I'm not a militant either. I keep my politics to myself. Why should I go in demanding this right or that? All they'll give me is the right to starve in the streets. I know what some people call me behind my back, and a few in public. I'm not a traitor to my race and I'll never be. But there's the smart and there's the unemployed."

"I'm a handsome man, women seem to go for my looks. Lots of beautiful young ladies of all stripes have thrown themselves at me. But I haven't touched anyone while sober since my wife died. So you're the first I've let come this close."

"I knew Jules before I met my husband. So it was easier to reconnect than

I thought. I've seen so little of him. It's more like slipping into an old habit. I know he doesn't love me. But the fantasy seemed to be something I thought I needed."

"But you don't need it now."

"Yes . . . but I don't know why."

"I'm why."

When the limousine stretched out in front of her apartment building, it caused a stir. The neighborhood kids, home from school, ran to see who hid behind the tinted windows. Eyes peeked from behind curtains, from verandas, and doors opened a crack. Boldly, the teenagers crowded the curb. Maureen climbed out alone to everyone's collective "Oh." Upstairs, she hurried out of her clothes and retreated to bed. TV proved poor company. She made herself read the latest bodice-ripper turning the pink-collar workforce red. She had to fight herself to keep from watching the clock. When the phone rang, she jumped it.

"Julian?"

"Dress to kill, Reeny. Be downstairs in twenty."

The evening was warm enough to get away without a wrap. He had been correct in his assessment. Her best feature was her total effect. He gasped when she stepped out onto the porch in answer to the chauffeur's knock. She lit the block in her high-necked, gold lamé mini-dress over glitter-laced bronze spandex and matching gold pumps. Large gold hoops looped her ears, accenting her gleaming kinky locks *au naturel*.

Inside the cabin, Julian smacked his lips and kissed at her.

"Reeny, you must be psychic."

"Huh?"

"We're color coordinated."

He was snazzed back in black-on-black accented with a thick yoke of eighteen-karat gold and a giant nugget friendship ring. She slid in next to him and he clutched her for a smooch-and-thrust.

"Don't want to muss you," he snorted heavily.

She patted her hairline then kicked back to relax as the limousine

35

flowed south along the Hollywood Freeway, ahead the Harbor–Santa Monica interchange, and the predominantly Afro-American reaches of South Central. His patter was buoyant and calculated to dispel ghosts.

"You need to leave that neighborhood, Reeny. The only thing worse than livin' among poor Blacks is livin' among poor immigrant Whites." He handed her a cigarette. She put it to her lips and he fired it with his platinum lighter.

"Not gold?" She teased.

"Expensive metals never clash. Remember that."

"Duly noted."

As she exhaled, he lit one for himself. "The director laid a half kilo of Mayan stoke on me."

"Damn, it's perfect-rolled. You don't do that often."

"When I'm not in a rush. Daddy taught me that, too. They called it locoweed in his day. Said everybody used to smoke it, grew wild everywhere, made common labor reserved for Niggahs and Injuns tolerable. Then, one day, some enterprising White Boy discovered the *real* reason colored folk were so happy under such miserable circumstances. Been illegal ever since. Here's your cut."

He slipped a fat lid into her gold-beaded clutch purse then busied himself pouring the champagne, playing the waiter, placing a cocktail napkin suggestively on her knee.

"How was that?"

"Wonderful. But we're not obligated to go through with this if we don't want to."

"Well, I want to, very much. But I have a confession to make."

"Oh?"

"Julian—he and I haven't seen each other since Winona's funeral. His image of me as a man is just that—his image. Unfortunately I'm not the man I once was."

"How so?"

"Like I said. Friends helped me get through those bad years. Good, generous folk who wouldn't let me destroy myself completely. Those drugs I used . . . they did some serious damage."

"You're impotent?"

* * *

"A toast?"

"Your turn, Reeny."

"To—to—the better man," she sputtered.

"Huh? What's *that* supposed to mean?"

"It just came to mind, Jules."

He caught a chill and shook.

"You *are* psychic. But you don't know how to make it work for you."
He took a gulp of bubbly. "That's what this evening is about. A man.
And it just so happens, he thinks he's a better man than me." He
rolled his eyes over her. "I want you to do me a favor."

"What kind of favor?"

"You know me, Reeny—I mean, you know my reputation as Mr.
Big Shit Actor. But you don't know where I come from." He topped
her glass then returned the magnum to its bucket. "Dred Scott and I
came from the same womb. I grew up in St. Louie, straddlin' that Big
Muddy some folk are so fond of praising in song. Those were the
strange fruit days, as Billie sang in the song, the years before civil
rights and all that guff. Black wasn't beautiful then—at all."

"I can get to that."

"Can you?" Briefly, he searched her eyes then retreated into memory. "My childhood—speakin' of my Daddy—was tough. He was a weak
man and a doomed man, but he did his damnedest by us. Twelve of us,
me being the youngest. My mother, bless her, died givin' birth to me."

He sighed.

"To make it short, I had a lot of pals in those days. We were all
eager to bust loose on the world, and, save a tragedy here or there, we
all made it. Despite the racists. We grew up, prospered, had our share
of troubles, women and good times. But this one boy—Maurice
Longstreet. His daddy was White. And no matter what, he never let
us forget it. It wasn't his high-tone skin, his gray eyes, or even his wavy
hair, more blond than brown. It was his superior attitude—his way of
constantly reminding us, since we were all darker-skinned, that he
was, by birth, somehow better—if not full-blooded. Because there were
things we had to take that he didn't. Understand?"

She nodded. "I was near out of high school before there was any such thing as freedom rides and boycotts. I can relate. But how come you stayed so tight if he was so color-struck?"

"Mud's thicker than blood. The others—well, they're scattered all over the globe. Me and Maurice went into the entertainment business together. Opened a club for a Harlem minute. Ripped and ran. And I thought all that old-timey niggah-shit was behind us. But it wasn't. It took a woman to show me it wasn't."

"She married him steada you."

He hissed. "Slow it down!"

"Just my uneducated guess," she smiled.

"Seriously, Maureen. I saw her first. I made her mine. I loved her. Maurice knew it. It made him jealous. He did everything he could to take her away from me. His White pappy could give him things my Black pappy couldn't give me. So he made better time, taking her fancy places, giving her expensive gifts. I was dirt poor. What could I offer?" His voice became a throaty whisper. "Not that she didn't deserve a man who could give her the world."

His eyes took in the passing view from behind tinted windows.

"They married. She was happy for awhile. Then that sorry mutha-fucka dogged her. She used to call me, cryin' when things got desper-ate. I tried my damnedest to talk her into leavin' him. But no matter how bad things got with Maurice, bein' the good Christian lady she was, she kept her marriage vows." He sighed. "She's a long time dead. Cancer. Maurice called me. One of the few decent things he's ever done. I flew down here in time to—to tell her I still loved her, before she died. Her name was Winona . . . Winona . . . O' Winona."

He repeated it in haunting whispers.

She searched his eyes. A glassiness cleared as quickly as it appeared. It was the only time she had ever heard him speak of love without a hint of ridicule.

Avoiding her stare, he took the joint hanging from his lower lip, studied it, took one last toke and crushed it in the armrest ashtray. She shrugged, wet the end of her roach, folded it into a cocktail napkin and tucked it inside her clutch. They were exiting onto the streets, the limousine taking the curves smoothly.

"So, Julian—what's the favor?"

"I want to show him up tonight. I want to take Maurice out on the town, spend goo-gobs of money, have a good time, and get him blasted. Then I want you to slay him."

"Beg your pardon?"

"He's never been able to get enough of fine brown frames. You're his weakness, Reeny. Maurice prides himself on seducing dark-skinned babes. The blacker the better. Maurice and me—we've always been rivals. He's always come out top dog. Now it's my turn to howl. I'm top dog, now. I want him to know it. And I want to see him know it."

"You said 'Slay him?'"

"He won't be able to resist you. Winona was tall, dark and classy. Like you. I'm gonna dangle you in front of him all night. Then, after we get back to his crib, I'll pretend to be drunk and flake out. I know Maurice. That's when he'll make his move. When it's over, I want you to tell me everything that happened, blow by blow."

She stared at him.

"I'm not a whore, Julian, if you ever bothered to notice."

He froze, looked at her strangely, then spoke deeply from within. "Of course you're not a whore."

"You're asking me to make love to a stranger."

"Once and only once."

"Julian—I was a wild child of the sixties too. But this is a little much."

"I'm asking you to help me answer a question that is driving me crazy. There is something I've *got* to know. And the only person who can give me that answer is you, Reeny."

"No jive," she said icily. She was beset by questions, confounded by this sudden intense and bizarre expression. She knew she was worthy of his trust, if he were being genuine, but could she trust him?

"Don't get me wrong, Reeny. No insult intended. I have the utmost respect for you."

This was another unexpected twist. What did this Maurice have that could drive the otherwise supercool Mr. Stoat to such extremes? Whatever he had, other than a light complexion, Julian was obsessed by it. While she was reluctant to do him this favor, she nevertheless found herself intrigued with the prospect of meeting Maurice. How often did one come across two men in love with the same ghost?

"I—I don't know, Julian."

"Please, Reeny. Pul-leeze." He put his champagne glass on the portable bar, bunched himself up, turned toward her, one knee shimmied to the floor in a half-kneel. He grabbed at her hands and held them to keep her from snatching them away. "I'll give you anything you want. Anything."

"That *would* make me a whore," she snapped.

He lowered his head then raised it so that his face glowed moonlike in the muted interior. His pain-filled tears burst, then streamed from his eyes. They rattled her. He was a consummate actor, she thought, but she did not know him well enough to tell if this were an act. It made her feel embarrassed for him and simultaneously aroused the urge to protect him.

"Maureen—I'm begging you to help me settle an old score."

"Alright, Jules."

"What!?" He stared in grateful wonder then blinked away tears. He took out a large white handkerchief, snotted into it and wiped his face. He put on his best puppy-dog face and bounced back onto the leather beside her. "Reeny, you're a champ!"

Immediately, she began to regret the choice, but now felt honor bound to see it through. Why, she asked herself, did she agree to do such a thing? What could she possibly prove to him by making such a sacrifice? Especially when he could not see it as precisely that? And what would she get for the trouble? She would be a few bills larger and could curl up in bed with all the dope she needed to fill his absence, if she bent that way. Mr. Stoat would fly back to San Francisco, happy as a fat black hawk, vengeance glowing in his beak.

He took her hand, raised it to his mouth, kissed it, and cooed. "Yeah—I'm a son-of-a-bitch. I know you love me, Reeny."

"I still enjoy the companionship of women. And the taste. I still have a mouth. Would you allow me to—taste your sweet lips?"

* * *

Maurice Longstreet had managed to acquire the mortgage on a modest elongated bungalow in one of the city's sedate palm-blessed enclaves in a formerly all-White residential area gone middle-class Black. The changeover was still recent in the city's history; the neighborhood retained its wholesome symmetry, with well-kept homes and freshly mown lawns along quiet, well-lit avenues. Blight had yet to settle in. There were no pedestrians visible or restless youths playing on the clean moonlit sidewalks. The limousine's arrival caused no stir, not even a raised curtain.

The driver held the doors as Julian made his grand exit, Maureen on his arm. He put a dip in his walk as he guided her toward the door, which swung open when they mounted the porch. They were greeted by a tall, big-boned man of medium build. His tan face was shadowy and bearded, long silver gray hair rippling back off his high forehead down his back in a loosely braided ponytail. His eyes were light gray with thick lids, sleek brows, and long feminine lashes. His nose was broad with flaring nostrils.

"Heyheyhey! Slip me some skin, Negro."

Maurice and Julian exchanged handshakes, cuffs to the shoulders, clasped one another and rocked.

"For ol' lang syne."

Maureen smiled and awaited her introduction.

"Who do we have here!" Maurice stepped back and checked her.

"Maurice, Maureen. How's that for alliteration?"

"Grammar aside, she's certainly speaks my lingo, *Daddio*."

"Dig—tonight's my treat. The limo's about to overheat, and I've picked a spot that can't be beat."

She shook her head and smiled at them.

"My jacket's right here. Let me lock this door and I'm set." Maurice reached in, snatched up a stylish black leather import and slipped into it as he tailed them to the limo. When the doors snugged shut, she found herself sandwiched between the two men who proceeded to yell their reunion in boyish joy without letup the entire ride.

"I didn't know how lonely I was, until this moment. . . ."

41

* * *

Nostalgia was first on the menu—over cocktails at the Sportsman. The trio was seated preferentially at a stage-side booth. One by one, a series of individual blues singers took the stage as the versatile band remarkably retooled for each.

"You shoulda seen that niggah run—barely able to get his pants over his legs. And me and Julian chased him into that cactus patch."

"His mama was pickin' needles out of his butt for a month!"

Went one reminiscence, told uproariously, about a college joe who had attempted to steal Winona's attentions.

"Remember that raggedy-ass chump beggin' us to let him go?"

"Some nerve. After he pulled that gun on us."

"The money was mine—won fair and square."

"Thought he could play us like a couple of hicks."

"Maurice snatched the gun right out of his hand. Man, you was a bold muthafucka. Coulda got us both eighty-sixed. Scared that booger's partners so bad they tore for the exits."

"Then we tied the sucka to the bed . . ."

". . . and whipped his ass bloody with an extension cord."

Went the adventure of a floating crap game gone wrong.

"Man, I thought they had us dead to rights."

"Those prison stripes appeared before my eyes. I knew we was headed for the chain gang—no doubt about it."

"If ol' lady Jefferson hadn't opened that door when she did we'd still be pickin' cotton and spadin' clay."

"'You boys get yo'selves inchere,' she said. To think—we used to be so scared of her we tiptoed whenever we had to pass her house."

"Never thought she was so kindly—or hip."

"She sure saved our bacon from bein' smoked."

Went the tale of how the neighborhood witch plucked them from the arms of lawmen after they had robbed a dry goods store.

"And ended our crime spree by tellin' our daddies. Remember *that*, Julian."

"She calls me Jules." He pointed at Maureen, glass in hand.

Bragging came next around the best table at Mr. Woodley's—over

42

club steaks and whiskey neat. A jazz quintet excelled at refreshing the old standards. Maurice graciously enjoyed his meal. Julian dropped his vegetarian pose and unloaded his recent accomplishments.

"They flew me to London then Istanbul, all expenses paid. Shooting on location. It's a wonderful way to travel with one's work. Celebrity is the great equalizer. I'm a Black man, yet accorded the greatest respect. Now that's what I call affirmative action!"

"Good for you, Jules. I haven't been anywhere but across town for years. I have to admit, I've never been as ambitious as you."

"If anyone had told you then that you'd end up being a studio musician, they would've had a fight on their hands."

"Very true."

"I heard that you'd hit the skids, if you don't mind my bringing up unpleasantries."

"Don't mind at all. I'm not ashamed to admit how much I depended on Winona. She was my heart." He stared into his plate. "It took me a long time to get myself back together–a very minor victory in the larger scheme of things."

"Last year I pulled down six figures, on the high end. A hundred times more than our daddies ever dreamed of makin' in a lifetime. Think of *that*."

"You did good, Jules. Proud of you."

Becoming wary of the situation, she noted that Mr. Longstreet's cool, unperturbed concessions were infuriating Mr. Stoat.

"I've won everything but an Oscar, and I'm working on that–got a new part I just auditioned for. A very sympathetic role."

"Knowing you, Jules, I'm sure you'll get that too."

She was not the referee, nor was she the prize. What was she to them? A witness? A judge? An audience, she decided.

"Young people, especially minorities, need to be exposed to real theatre, like they've got on the East Coast. That's why I established my workshop. We've purchased a building near the Presidio. It's my legacy to the city."

"You've become quite the upstanding citizen." Maurice said it without a hint of envy. "Proud of you, Jules," he repeated.

There was a lull over the table as Maurice became deeply intro-

43

JAZZ & TWELVE O'CLOCK TALES

spective. She caught a look of smug cynicism in Julian's eyes. He signaled her with a slight nod.

"Jules—I haven't amounted to much over these years. It's a painful thing to acknowledge. But I can honestly say I haven't any regrets except perhaps one."

Eagerly Julian leaned forward mid-chew, fork and knife paused. "And what is that?"

Maurice eyed him. "That Winona and I never had children."

Julian blanched then reddened, livid.

Quickly, Maureen stood and took Maurice by the hand. "Look, you two have ignored me all evening. How about a spin?"

Maurice read her intention, laid his napkin aside and allowed himself to be led away. At foxtrot tempo, he took the lead as they joined the couples on the dance floor. Julian stared after them before returning his attention to his plate.

"You're a smart girl, Maureen."

"Thank you. You're pretty smart yourself. You know exactly what he's doing."

"Yes. But why stop him? A man's got to have his fun."

"Even at your expense?"

"It's not costing me a dime."

"That's not what I mean."

"Or a drop of sweat. Although, if he had pulled this twenty years ago, I would've invited him into the alley."

They exchanged smiles. Maurice took in her face, the curve of her neckline. He nestled his nose under her ear and inhaled.

"Ahhh. Quite a beauty. I know Jules. You're the one who's paying."

"Touché."

He danced her back to their table.

Not to be outclassed, Julian stood and bowed, took her hand and helped her into her seat, pretending to have recovered his humor.

"You two make quite a pair," he winked at her.

Maurice pretended not to notice.

Jokes and amusing stories signaled the next phase on a hop through the Parisian Room for more jazz. Julian knew the master of ceremonies and was up and about the room socializing, seeming to drink heavily, buying drinks all around while Maureen and Maurice sat thoughtfully and watched, talking softly under the music. This time, Julian's act was eerily convincing.

"Does he usually drink that heavily?"

"Not that I've ever seen."

"As a reformed drunk, it's not pretty to watch."

"You love him, don't you."

"Like a brother. And too much to be a party to this."

"He wants to show you a good time."

"That's no way to do it."

When Julian finally returned to the table, Maurice made a show of noting the time. "It's late my friend. In my new decrepitude, I've become an early riser."

"Par-ty poop-oop-per—sonofabitch." Julian grinned broadly, stretching his face, rolling his eyes. "What say, Maureen?"

She nodded reluctantly. He was so good an actor, she didn't know whether he was actually drunk or not.

"Then—back to Maurice's joint, for a nightcap. Huh?" He sprang up, tilted sideways and collapsed onto the floor. The bouncer and the manager helped carry him outside and wedged him into the limousine. He lolled on the leather seat opposite them and they sat in silence, glaring at their prostrate host. As they pulled in front of the house, Julian unexpectedly returned to consciousness.

"I'm not drunk!" he protested, as Maurice tried to talk them out of coming inside. "A little tipsy—that's all."

He spun up the walkway, leaning against Maureen for support. She could tell by his shift in body weight that he was sober and keeping up his act. For a moment, she had hoped that an honest way out had presented itself. She liked Maurice, found him attractive, and regretted having agreed to Julian's ugly scheme. She was a woman of her word. If she had to go through with it, she would—as foolish as she now felt.

Toward the evening's end, she had begun to feel Winona's presence. Maureen understood how she had loved two very different men, yet had married the one. She now understood Winona's choice. She also accepted the obvious—that her favor to Julian would not deepen their relationship. When this night was over, she would never hear from or see either man again.

"I'll be damned. I knew that rascal was up to something. I couldn't figure out what it was. Imagine him wanting to pull a stunt like that on me."

"I agreed to go through with it—but I hadn't met you. Now that I have— well, I can't be party to such a dirty trick. I like you, I love him. How do I please him and keep what little self-respect I have left?"

"You know he's going to dump you, don't you?"

"Yes."

"I feel for you. You're a beautiful thing. Young enough to get over the likes of us. So, here's what you do . . ."

Inside, the house was roomy, warm, and cozy. There was an upright piano on one wall with sheets of music scattered about. A saxophone case stood on a stand next to it. Two sofas made an ell that doubled as a room divider. There was a large lace-covered mahogany table in the center of the dining area, a built-in breakfront with shelves, and an old Singer sewing machine at a window.

Julian insisted on nightcaps and grew petulant when Maurice tried to refuse.

"What kind of hospitality is that, after I've taken you out. When was the last time anybody bought you a steak dinner? Besides, I'm not driving."

"If you insist."

"I insist."

When Maurice disappeared down the hallway toward the kitchen, Julian leapt up, grabbed her and happily smacked her on the lips. "How'm I doin', Reeny?"

"You even had me fooled."

"Told you I'm a damned good actor. This is better than an Oscar!"

"What now?"

"Hang tight. I'm gonna do my *Camille* bit. Then the rest is up to you."

At the sound of Maurice's steps, Julian instantly reverted to a state of clownish inebriation. "Maureeece, my man! What have ya got!"

46

"I don't keep hard liquor around. Just this white wine."

"Dat'll do, dat'll do!"

Dutifully, Maurice filled three wineglasses.

"I pro-poz a toast!"

"Sure, go ahead Jules."

"To friends and lovers!"

They touched rims. Julian slurped his down in an exaggerated guzzle, then began to choke and gag—making a disgusting dribble down his chin and onto his chest. He went suddenly rigid and collapsed on the sofa behind him. Maureen reached for the napkins, rushed to his side, and dabbed away the slobber. Maurice was genuinely shocked and stared at them. Suddenly, Julian began to snort and snore as if he'd fallen into a drunken sleep. Maurice doffed his jacket and covered him. Then he took Maureen by the elbow, quietly pulling her away, speaking in whispers.

"The driver's cool for the night. I think we should let him sleep. He looks like an overgrown kid, doesn't he?"

She nodded, certain she detected a smile under all that snoring.

"Come on. We'll spend the night in here."

He took her by the elbow, opened the door to his bedroom and guided her in. It was ordinary but nice—with a rug over the hardwood floor and homemade curtains. There was a dressing table with a small bench and a rocking chair. The queen-sized bed was neatly made, pillows piled high. Her eyes fell instantly on the dresser and a portrait of a smiling young couple. Maurice turned on the bedside lamp. "Winona and me," he said. "Be right back."

She reached for the gold-framed photograph, unable to keep her hands from touching it. She shivered. She was identical to the woman smiling blissfully next to Maurice, and into her eyes. Winona resembled Maureen enough to be a twin with pressed hair. Her eyes seemed more birdlike, her hair longer and wavier, and she had a slight overbite. But to the uneducated eye, Winona and Maureen had the same face and complexion.

"My God," she hissed.

Dazzedly, she looked at the worn upholstered rocking chair, peered out the curtains onto a tiny patch of poorly watered lawn revealed by the street lamp. She was settling on the edge of the bed, head still spinning, when Maurice returned, bottle and wineglasses in hand. What was she going to do?

"He's snoring up a storm out there. I gave him a good shaking, just to make sure he's sound asleep." He smiled, his eyes taking her in anew. He freshened their drinks.

"Jules takes good care of himself," she said lamely. "This has been unlike him."

"Never mind him. Let's think of us, now. A toast." He stood before her.

"Okay. To what?"

"How about—with hand and heart, thought and word, we meet on the path of beauty." He gazed at her, radiating warmth, tenderness and the hunger her resemblance to Winona had awakened.

"Ahh." She was too moved to smile.

They touched glasses, drank, then Maurice closed the bedroom door and joined her on the bed. She inhaled dramatically, then told Maurice about Julian's plot and explained why she was there. He was receptive and amused. They talked as friends, propped up on the pil-lows, until sleepiness overtook them. Other than Julian, their best conversation was a mutual sharing of grief and woes of having lost lovers to death. The emotional exchanges were heavy, yet they felt light and lifted of burdens. They ended their unravelings in a grateful kiss goodnight. He thanked her for the truth, left her the bed, took the extra quilt, and slept fitfully in the rocking chair.

The smell of fresh brewed coffee woke Maureen. She searched the unfamiliar dimness. Squinting at the alarm clock, she realized it was six in the morning. She threw back the covers, leapt from the bed and slipped into her pantyhose and bra. There was a gentle knock and then the door opened. Maurice entered, carrying a steaming mug.

"I thought you could use this."

"Yes, thanks."

"If you'd like, the shower's all yours."

"I'd better not. I've got to get home in time to clean up, change, and go to work."

"There's a cup like this one on the dining room table, if you want to rouse Jules, the son-of-a-gun. I'll go out front and jam the chauffeur."

As soon as Maurice stepped through the front door, Julian leapt to his feet, grabbed her by the arms, and bounced with delight.

"Was that an Academy Award performance or was it, Reeny? I thought I was gonna die when he covered me with his jacket. I almost busted out laughin'. What a scream!"

"I thought it was kinda sweet."

He looked a bit contrite. "Yeah. I guess."

She shook her head and pushed the mug at him. "I thought you had actually gotten drunk. Better drink this. You're supposed to have a hangover."

"Yeah, that's right. Okay."

"I've got to be at work, Jules. It's still the middle of my week."

"Umm—okay. We'll say a quick goodbye."

Maurice returned as they choked down the last of the hot coffee. Julian's demeanor changed instantly as his knees trembled and his hand went to the back of his neck.

"Ooooooh, boy. Did we party, or did we party?"

"We partied. And now it's time to party yourself on outta here," Maurice smiled, took Maureen in his arms and kissed her. She kissed back. They lingered meaningfully, arm-in-arm, then parted. "I had a great time."

Julian smiled happily. "I see you two hit it off while I was passed out! Man—what a friend you turned out to be, stealin' my woman the minute my back is turned!"

"We're just acquaintances, that's all. Right, Maureen?"

"Right." She smiled and followed the tug of Julian's hand as he pulled her away. He put his hand to her waist and licked her lips with his huge crimson tongue.

Maurice made a wry little smile.

"Look, Reeny's got that job of hers," Jules croaked, "and I've got a plane to catch. So we're gonna take a rain check on breakfast. How's about that?"

"Cool with me, Jules. You always know where to find me, if and when." He walked them to the door. As they stepped onto the porch,

Maurice caught her eyes. His glance was knowing and sympathetic.

She went ahead of Julian, leaving the old buddies to exchange last words and handshakes. Maurice watched and waved from the porch as Julian skipped after her and dove into the backseat. As they pulled away from the curb, he broke into uproarious laughter. He reached into his jacket pocket, pulled out a wad of cash and a vial of cocaine. He took her clutch, unzipped it, stuffed the goodies inside, zipped it and plopped it into her lap.

"This'll go good with the smoke. I always pay my debts, Reeny." He looked at her expectantly.

She lowered her eyes and looked at her lap, holding her pose to set the moment. Julian wasn't the only one who could act. Then she raised her eyes to meet his gaze.

"So what happened?"

"You were right about him." Her eyes glistened. "He did just what you said he would. He wanted me . . . and we . . ."

"You what? C'mon!"

"We talked a while, to get to know each other. Then—we made love," she lied, struggling with the sudden impulse to laugh.

"You damned near fucked him to death, tell me!"

"I went down on him," she pursed her lips and licked out her tongue.

"Whoooowhee! Hah!"

"He was terribly excited and wanted me."

"How many times," he rocked.

"Twice," she stretched the lie.

"Shitttttt. What—about fifteen, twenty minutes each?"

"No—much longer than that. He's quite a lover, after a fashion."

"Oh, he is—huh?" His nares flared, his eyes assaulted her.

She nodded, returning his gaze evenly.

"But was he as *good* a lover as me?"

"No. No, he wasn't. Almost."

"Almost?" He closed his eyes and savored it. "A beautiful word if I ever heard one." Beyond a smile, his face broke into an uncanny crack. He leaned forward, plucked the half-truth from her eyes then fell back and shuddered in ecstasy.

"Oh, Reeny—*that's* what I've waited half a lifetime to hear."

Julian offered kisses but no promises. He took off her shoes and kissed and chewed her stockinged feet throughout the journey, singing "almost," stretching and elongating the word as if it were a jazz refrain. Maurice had been right, she mused, Julian was a study in smugness. She loathed the weakness he aroused in her. Curiosity had solved the mystery of the great love of his life, but now what? It was a love she resembled but with which she could never compete.

If success were the best revenge, and living well second best, then deception was a close third. Maureen was discharged at her apartment building door. The limousine hovered curbside until she disappeared inside, then it sped away. Upstairs, she emptied the contraband into the trash, tossed her clutch purse into a whatnot drawer. She regretted keeping even one cent of Julian's money, but she was terribly broke despite the regular paydays, and her creditors would be happy men tomorrow. It was time to find a better-paying situation.

Mindful of the hour, she showered, knowing she could tough it through. It would take a couple of weeks before knowing looks from coworkers went blank and the gossip died down. She dressed slowly, deliberately taking more time than needed, inward thoughts roiling in the conflicts aroused by images of Julian, Maurice, and that ghost of theirs, Winona.

It didn't take a shrink to figure out Winona's choice. She loved both men. But she had chosen the gallant Maurice over the meanly selfish Julian. Maurice did have his weaknesses. But his kindness and generosity, his willingness to set his own needs aside for the sake of others, even to appease an old buddy's ego, were rare and admirable qualities, if on the lowest levels where Julian chose to play. Julian was the type of man who needed strong opposition to stay strong himself. It would have hurt him to discover that the rival he imagined existed only in his imagination. Too, Maurice had been right. Indeed—there was a perverse kind of satisfaction in lying to a liar.

As she groped for a matched set of earrings, she heard a whisper. *All is forgiven, Babe. Forgive yourself.*

That old snapshot of Rusty, framed and placed next to her jewelry box, caught her eye. He smiled up at her from underneath the hood of his uncle's truck, where she had caught him on camera. His forehead was smeared with grease, white teeth catching sunlight. She kissed its glassy surface then held it close. Here she was, cheated by circumstances into living their future alone. That he was there for her, in the past, steeled her against self-pity. At the least she was alive, therefore, salvage and salvation were possibilities. If she would let him, she realized suddenly, *if she let him*, the best of Rusty, who survived in her memories, would become her strength.

Always, Babe . . . always . . .

Backcity
Transit
by Day

I GUESS I WANDERED senselessly from the platform, near as I can figure. But my memory has returned. Vividly. Following the dictates of habit, I must have boarded this city bus, which will, in the next five minutes, deposit me on the corner of the block where I rent my modest apartment. As soon as I enter my front room door, I will seize the remote control unit, turn on the television, and watch the early afternoon newscasts. I'm certain this horrible incident that has caused my temporary blank-out will be the special report on every local station.

I knew I was in trouble when the alarm went off this morning. I could not get up. I hit the snooze button five times before I finally drug myself from beneath the queen-sized comforter. It was tough facing the morning's chill, tough forcing my recalcitrant feet across the icy bathroom tiles, tough ridding my head of the residue of interrupted dreams.

Nevertheless, the demands of body and wallet prevailed, I had to be at work on time, and the bus would not wait. Riders are scarce in those frosty hours before the rush. Mine is a professional-class residential area where only the maids, the decrepit, and the adolescent ride the bus during peak hours. Odd worker out, I usually find myself rattling around in it alone, except for the driver, until we reach the tiny mall at the heart of this little bedroom enclave hidden sedately within the sprawling anus of Los Angeles.

Standing in the cool, early morning drizzle, I'm pleased to lower my umbrella and climb aboard, my fare buried in the palm of my gloved left hand so that I don't have to go into my purse. The conk-haired, mocha-skinned driver stares hard at me as I nervously slip the bill into the vacuum slot and drop in the necessary coins. I hear his question, but it's none of his business what I'm doing in the neighborhood, why I'm wearing such expensive sunglasses on a rainy day, that he didn't know Black people lived in this area, and otherwise I'm not in the mood to talk to strangers.

"Blue line, green line," I sing.

He gives me a transfer and I slip it neatly into my glove. I have a right to be eccentric. I take the seat directly behind the driver's cubby so that I don't have to be bothered by his nose. I make a mental note to buy that monthly boarding pass as soon as possible so I can give up my evening ritual of organizing loose change and singles.

Tada! In minutes, I exit the familiar bus, feeling the driver's eyes on my behind. But my thoughts are on my next connection, the city's first real tramway. It's been open for well over a year but still feels new. My first trip on the metro rail was better than expected. The Nippon-style trams zip along quietly compared to a bus. Like those sci-fi comic book tramways. All metal and Plexiglas as translucent as clean dishwater. Not at all like the old red cars of my childhood, smelling of oil, smoke, and axle grease. There's no smell these days, except what drifts in on the air from outside, the sweaty stink of other passengers or the artificial lemony twinge of industrial cleaning solvents. As I ride, it's difficult to remain awake. All noises are dull except for the distant clang of the warning lights, the strangely correct honk of the train itself as a station is approached, and the electronic buzzer that signals the openings and closings of passenger doors. Everything is diffuse, spotless and hushed, all silvery grays, muted whites, and unobtrusive blues.

(Someone is staring at me. I do not allow them to draw my eyes. Having a young face is not always a blessing.)

I find it so easy to lose consciousness, nodding with the gentle shimmy of the over-ground people mover. Mercifully, none of that tepid pop-rock brood music is piped into the cars. One is left to one's thoughts, provided one is not seated sideways so that one's ear is assaulted by the loud smacking of insensitive bitchy jaws on a monstrous wad of chewing gum, the intramural sports babblings of macho enthusiasts of "the game," the rantings of a deranged street hustler, or a colic-and-scream spewing mink-haired infant raging to escape from the stroller that has just rolled over one's foot.

The majority of the passengers all seem to be undergoing the same process of being lulled into mild catatonic pose: the breath becomes shallow, the posture frozen, the eyes introspective, the jaw relaxed, the arms limp and sinewless as one is whizzed work-ward, schoolward, to whatever destiny unreels. Getting there incrementally.

And this, too, infects me as I stare without focus at the passing landscape which, with the exception of a shopping mall or two, is a depressing spectacle of dilapidated pastel A-frames and gritty-gray public housing projects with shabby roofs, junk-filled lawns, unmendable fences, and dented primer-splatted jalopies blooming on the blacktop. These are neighborhoods I once knew and cannot forget. Watching carefully, I can almost taste the mornings as they were then: the resonant repetitions of engines marginally turning over; the fresh drizzle settled on windshields and windows, evaporating with the sun's easterly warming; the aromas of hot cereals, cheap coffee, greasy sausages, and burnt Nucoaed toast; the broad avenues dotted with meandering clumps of dark children, reluctantly headed schoolward; the solitary, elderly churchwomen with their heavy-handled totes on their ways to tend the sick and shut-ins or the preschoolers of young working class couples.

I knew such a woman. She cared for me as a child.

What I remember most about her was how the yellows of her ancient Honduran eyes lit up when she was surprised. And how I delighted in causing that expression by making mischief. Her pressed red-brown hair was always perfect-kept in a fine brown hair net. And now that I think of it, I enjoyed how, when she got especially angry, she'd forget herself and curse in a mix of Spanish and an Africanized native dialect I loved and laughed to hear. I remember my fascination with her ringless fingers as she quick-iced the high layers of her home-baked butter cakes. I remember the bronze, red, and gold silk shawl she prized with its elegantly fine fringe. She wore it over her shoulder on brisk, fall mornings or wrapped around her broad, high hips on special occasions. And I remember that she kept her man when most women her age always seemed to be alone, in mourning.

A stop is called and my reverie snaps. The ghost dispelled is replaced by a vision of cement structures rising and falling across a palm-dotted distance.

My stop always comes up too soon.

Now my workday has ended, as has the return trip on the crowded bus that jerked to a slam at the intersection before the metropolitan blue line station, causing me to brace myself by jamming the tip of my damp umbrella into a gap between a neighboring seat and a Latino student's booted foot. Everyone rushes the exit, knowing the north-bound tram is due. I'm exhausted and barely able to follow them as they wade against traffic, ignoring the red stoplight, forcing eager automobile drivers to slam on brakes. The tram arrives as I waddle up the access ramp, my feet aching, protesting with every step of my pricey wedgies as I join the late-day swarm.

No seats are available except the ones that make the rider face backward, in the direction from which they've just come. I wonder what idiot bureaucrat on antidepressants approved this design.

Invariably, the train crosses the awesomely engineered cement river, the slight flow of water indistinguishable except on sunny days when the light catches it proper or when heavy rains send it brimming high, choppy and wide. On certain walls, on underpasses, and in some daringly remarkable spots, taggers have spray-painted defiant graffiti on all available space. Without my specs, I'm unable to interpret any of it. But the steady clip of the tram causes the images to flow together in a momentary visual dance.

As my mid-transit stop approaches, I force myself out of the narrow seat designed to marginally contain my mass, shift my purse so that it's snug under my left arm, grip my umbrella, and follow the crowd out, down, and around to the escalator rising toward the inter-secting green line. There's a deputy uniformed in matching pants and jacket, brass star radiant on his chest. He asks to see my ticket. I extend my left palm forward and peel back the glove. He peeps, nods, and I move on.

I envision myself standing on the westbound side, as I grasp the rail and mount the step rising skyward. In two blinks it seems I'm there, wading through the crowd, looking for a place to sit. But it's late afternoon. The few precious green and blue benches and those clunky immobile stone chairs are fully occupied. I find a pale green post to lean against for the five minutes I know it will take before the train arrives.

It is at this moment that I'm overpowered by the urge for a drink of coffee, tea, or chocolate—a wet hotness steaming upward toward my brow, fogging my tinted lenses. A futile search for anything resem-bling a vending machine reveals signs stating that no food or drinks are allowed on the platform, that everyone must have a ticket, and that the Country Sheriff's department is now responsible for security on the platform. My thirst is awful, and I struggle to moisten my throat, imagining the cool sweet high-caloric contents of my little refrigerator. I have a flask in my purse, but to risk a swig might prove embarrass-ing if not illegal.

To distract myself from the wait and my thirst, I survey my sur-roundings. I recognize several double life-size sculptures, designed on the old pickaninny theme. I'd seen them earlier, placed in strategic spots, some of the figures mounted high on the cement walls, most of them placed playfully as if potential passengers themselves. I know the work of this Californian artist, a Black man who has fused his Legba-like sensibility with the expressionism of Dubuffet and a clever overlay of Chagall. I'm struck by the irony of my observation, doubt any of the passengers appreciate the decades of thought underscoring these artworks, let alone the monumental confluences of history that have created the very platform on which we stand and have brought us to this stepping-off point.

As I inwardly pursue the convolutions of my knowing, my eyes focus on one particular pickaninny whose head is shaped to suggest it has thick braided hair echoed in the shapes of the cartoon-like hands that hide its grotesquely cute facelessness. Two children, the color of paper bags, with that sandy gray-colored hair suggestive of a White grandparent, step into my line of vision. They are darling, the boy about seven, the girl about six and nearly his twin. The boy holds their tickets in his left hand, wondrously touches and strokes the giant female pickaninny with his right hand. His sister is also enthralled by the figure. They circle it, smile at it and each other. Then they turn abruptly and resume their horseplay, darting in and out between the other passengers. Peripherally, I look around. Isn't there an adult keeping an eye on them? A mother who might be preoccupied with a teething infant or distracted by a travel-sick toddler? Perhaps an unemployed father, the day's involuntary babysitter. Or an older brother or sister. It is a cool sunny day despite the periodic fall rain. These children should have coats on over their thin blue polyester rags to protect their skinny little limbs.

How fast does it take to have such thoughts? To internally chide the absent parent for allowing their children to travel alone under such dangerous conditions? I notice that like the subways in Manhattan, there's nothing but common sense and sure footing between the platform and the rail below.

Suddenly, I hear the clang that accompanies the warning lights as the eastbound tram on the other side of the platform arrives, passengers exit and enter, and in seconds it's gone. I go back to my own preoccupation with nothing, notice two warning signs painted on the concrete, one in Spanish and, a few feet away, in English. I amuse myself by silently sounding out the Spanish. Now, I hear the clang that accompanies the arrival of the westbound tram. I see its shadowy form through the mesh of the freeway divider as it rounds the curb and that halogen cyclops eye shimmers like a beacon. But my eyes are drawn quickly to my right, not more than two yards away.

Those same two children are at the platform ledge. The boy has lifted his sister by her waist and is dangling her over the edge. I am not the only one who sees this. A tall sepia man in a leather tam, matching trousers, and a white long-sleeved shirt, races toward them, his arms outstretched, his mouth opened in a shout. From another angle, a yelling blond White man in his thirties rushes toward them, his arms likewise outstretched.

The boy is on tiptoes, his gray-tinged head resting against the small of his sister's back just as his grip fails. She drops through the chute of his arms. And his arms fly skyward and dangle there, clawing heaven, high above his head, which is jerked downward, his mouth gaped as wide as the smile on that faceless pickaninny.

The swoosh of the approaching tram is a roar between my ears above the moans and screams of shocked witnesses. People are rushing about the tram, on and off it. Someone jostles me backward and I recognize the contorted face of the deputy as he wades through the knot of onlookers. I turn away. An old Mexican woman faints in front of me. Someone kicks her purse open as he stumbles over her.

It's all blank after that.

I estimate that nearly an hour of my day was lost. Up until that moment ago when I awoke on the bus, jarred back into my skin by the hydraulic hiss of doors snapping open then shut in mid-traffic. The ribs of my umbrella were fairly embedded in my right hand. There was the annoying awareness that my purse strap was strangling my left shoulder. Its bulk was uncomfortable in my lap. I open it now to see if I lost anything in my confusion. My doeskin eyeglass case is open and empty. I plow fruitlessly for my sunglasses until I remember I'm still wearing them. No, all the contents are here. Lucky me, nothing is missing. Nothing was lost in the panic.

Nothing at all.

Purgatory

SEARCH. DETOX. HOLDING.

This, here, is my bedevilment.

Sergeant Stubbs tersely informed me that I would have to come down for a screening. "We don't just accept anyone," he said in response to my query about turning myself in. I was worried all through the questionnaire; I was asked such intimate questions. The one that struck me as oddest was whether I was homosexual or bi-sexual. I stated flatly that I was hetero, although I was left wondering what the consequences might have been if I had answered otherwise.

Admittance to the new slams is like partial rent for a month or a half dozen meals at a chichi restaurant. You pay to do an easy stretch in a clean environ where the only sounds are the low but steady buzz of a generator encased in cement and hidden from view, and the distant muted tones of voices real or electronic, automatic bolts being released, the leather scruffings of deputized feet, sounds similar to the echoes heard leaving the shower of a high school gym.

One of the values in paying for your own imprisonment is that you don't have to be exposed to crazies. There's a certain element of decorum to be found here distinctly lacking in county facilities. Someone occasionally manages a please or a thank you.

As I'm waiting to be searched, two FBI agents in their mid-thirties arrive to pick up an inmate for transport. I'm surprised at their size: not that I'm so tall, but that they're short. Their "package" is certainly bigger than they are; of course they're armed and perhaps well trained in some martial art. The object of their quest is in the holding tank one wall over and stares at me through the glass, hands in pockets, eyes blank. He looks like a case of white-collar crime, is in his late fifties, dressed in an ordinary striped shirt, slacks, loafers, jacket. His graying blond hair is uncombed. Before I can watch them process him, Deputy Debbie steers me to the fingerprinting desk.

This is considered unit E. The decor is done in eggshell white, a split-level affair. The stairs are solid blue as are the doors. I pen this on the scratched surface of a giant table, a hexagonal bud of solid steel with four, round, hammerhead petals that serve as stools. This unit houses four cells, two upstairs and two down. There's a telephone that takes no coins, a charge phone. You enter your number and the mechanized operator instructs you that you may make collect calls only and to remain on the line until your call is completed; you can press another combination of buttons if you wish to hear her message in Spanish. Two signs on the wall adjacent to the phones offer free bail review, one English, the other Español.

The classic bars are obsolete. As near as I'm able to assess, this section of the jail is built on the beehive principal. The observation tower is reduced to a video monitoring station at its core. This odd hexahedral mini-courtyard, site of my incarceration, is also the TV room and, like each cell, is controlled by the electronic bolt system. There's an intercom plate located near each door. You are allowed to leave your cell door open so that you may come and go. You press a mill-sized button to communicate with the sentry at video center. He controls everything from where he sits—the doors, the lights, the television set, and the intercom units.

The odd-shaped wall opposite the cells consists of the door itself and thick three-by-three panes of bulletproof glass (when I'm searched,

Deputy Debbie rolls her eyes and tells me I'd be surprised at the things women can get "up there," including guns) encased in steel mullions, a wall of steel and cement, fifteen feet from floor to ceiling. The outer wall of each cell is likewise constructed, with an opaque square of translucent color at the base pane of the cell, adjacent to the bed, next to the door. I can't figure out the function of the opacity since it provides no concealment for the sleeping inmate. The doors of each cell are painted blue, the ID numbers stenciled in large eggshell white letters. My cell is E13.

I can barely see across the corridor to where the men are housed. I can see the video station more clearly and the guard on duty as he moves about, drinks coffee, or reads a newspaper.

I'm given a slipcover sheet, top sheet, pillow and case, two towels, a rough-napped dark gray blanket, and a neon orange jumpsuit as my issue. I'm instructed that I may wear my regular clothes while in the unit but am to wear the jumpsuit at all times when outside the unit.

I'm alone now and in my neon orange jumpsuit. I think this thing looks ridiculous on me. It puts emphasis on my thickening waist and broad hips. I'm the color of Halloween: black socks, black hair, black bra, and black panties underneath. Brown skin. I'm allowed to keep all my property including my watch, even the book and the pen. If I had known they were so lenient here I would've brought a dozen pens. I don't know how long it will be before this one runs out of ink.

Outside it is fall. Inside here it is summer.

Deputy Jane instructs me in my new routine. First stop she assists me with is the laundry. I'm shown how to operate the front-loading washer and dryer. A concentrated liquid detergent is used, fabric softener and bleach for the white things. As we put away an early wash, she tells me about a thirty-two-year-old prostitute who didn't know how to fold sheets and how that "sure pissed me off. You'd think the one thing a hooker'd know how to fold is sheets." The edge in her voice tells me this little woman could be dangerous if incited. She is armed with a gun holstered at her hip, as are all the assistant deputies. They all sport blackjacks and hand-sized walkie-talkies that clip to their utility belts.

I don't tell her I like to fold sheets.

I'm reminded of how I used to wash and fold diapers for my baby brother. I'd help Mama carry the baskets out to the clothesline in the back yard, behind the garage. I'd hand her the wet things so she wouldn't have to bend. Sometimes she got dizzy when she bent over. Mama would go into her bright orange clothespin bag, take a couple between her teeth and a bunch in her right hand and snap those diapers to attention, one-by-one, overlapping at the ends so that one clothespin held two in place. In minutes they would be drinking in sunshine. Afterwards, as I gathered and folded them I felt the solar warmth against my arms. I hugged them to my face as if, somehow, love as well as light had been captured in the cloth.

While the sheets and towels are washing, Deputy Jane takes me to the kitchen, one door down. The kitchen has top-notch institutional equipment, a walk-in freezer, a giant refrigerator, garbage disposal, microwave oven, and coffeemaker. I meet Deputy John and Deputy Milton, both Blacks, as they prepare a snack. Deputy Jane is a nice, blonde White woman in her mid-thirties. They all seem to be about the same age. She shows me how to prepare lunch and dinner for the inmates. TV dinners. Like home.

At four-thirty every morning they wake me to prepare mess. Before food is prepared the prisoner count is given to determine how many bowls will be set out or trays popped into the massive institutional oven. Meals are served at six, twelve, and six. They get one cup of milk made from powder for breakfast. Orange juice, tea and coffee are for the staff only. Inmates get one cup of lemonade made from a powdered mix, one with lunch and one with dinner. I may have my choice of prisoner or staff food, whatever I want.

Breakfast consists of sugar-frosted cornflakes, a half-cup of fruit, and one stingy cup of milk. I fill each bowl with flakes, usually emptying several boxes. I get to keep the prizes. Then I pour the milk, prepared the night before, into paper cups. Lastly, I prepare the fruit, which is actually half of a canned cling peach with a splash of juice. The one feeble plastic spoon, to be used for the meal, is then placed in each serving.

For the big meals I go into the freezer and select an entree: pasta or beans for lunch. There's meat (loaf or chopped steak), chicken, or

63

fish for dinner. I remove the little trays and stab holes in the clear plastic wrap covers after I peel away the plastic flap covering the dessert section. Then I pop them into the preheated oven as instructed. The steaming dinners are taken from the oven and the remaining cellophane stripped away, risking burns when there are more than twenty. I'm allowed to have a "hungry sucka," a large TV dinner with twice the meat entree, if I want, and even ice cream. The other inmates can only have the regular sized din-dins and no dessert except what's on that tray. They also get a double packet of saltine crackers, two crackers per packet, placed atop the veggie section. A tiny plastic spoon is the only utensil allowed, and it's anchored in the meat or pasta. When the dinners are finally prepped they're placed on trays and the trays are placed in the cart. The desk sergeant is notified when grub is ready.

The food cart is accompanied by an officer who checks each unit and rounds up the inmates. Then the steward, usually me, hands each individual their meal, one by one, through the lock-controlled, hinged, eight-inch by one-foot slot set in a wide belly-level mullion. The only meal I don't serve is breakfast. I haven't figured out the reason for that yet. Maybe it's to give one of the male inmates a break. Maybe it's to keep me from developing an overblown sense of self-importance.

Outside of the initial run-through, my housekeeping duties are unmonitored. If the kitchen door is locked I may request the key from the desk sergeant. I'm allowed to come and go from the kitchen as I please as long as I don't abuse the privilege. There's no place to sit, but I can stay in it as long as I want. I wash all the dishes. Sometime within the hour-and-a-half to two hours it takes to prepare each meal and clean up, I eat.

Two prisoners have been released and so there are two extra meals and two extra lemonades to be shared. Later I learn the women deputies are the only ones who'll allow the inmates any extras—like if I prepare thirty-six meals and a half dozen inmates are released before dinner. When my police escort is female, prisoners get something extra. When my escort is male they strictly get the one tray allotted.

There's a key-operated slot through which each inmate is handed his food and drink. I didn't notice it before, but there's a like slot near the door in my unit. My nine-by-twelve designer cell consists of a stone futon with a mattress of stitched light gray-green plastic, a solid combination steel commode, sink, and water fountain. Theoretically there's hot and cold running water but each comes out only in thirty-second spurts in response to the button pushed; therefore, there's only cold water. Above the sink hangs a steel-on-alloy mirror that reflects my resignation.

The only serious drawback to internship in the new slams is the thorough lack of privacy. There's a camera in each cell that scans the entire space. I can be seen even when I take a squat. The male guards can watch me as much as they please. As can anyone coming to the door of the unit. Nothing is concealed. Not even the indignity of wiping one's behind. The phosphorescent lamps are elongated triangles mounted to the nine-foot ceiling, one directly across from my bunk, the other on the opposite wall over the mirror. There's a fire sprinkler and smoke alarm. The cell floor is painted gray.

I've never seen or heard of the cockroach or rat that could get in or out of here. This place is so sterile dust doesn't even collect. In its own right, it's a space capsule.

While feeding the male inmates, I noticed one cell contained several boom boxes. I assumed long-term prisoners were housed there though I saw no one. Perhaps they were all outside on work detail. After being here less than twenty-four hours I missed my music. I listen to music constantly when at liberty: stereo radio, the compact disc and cassette player, at clubs.

When I finish with my housekeeping duties I return to my cell. I think about my lover as I sit there. I tried to call him awhile ago but he wasn't home yet. He didn't sleep well the last night we were together for worry about me. I heard him up about five o'clock in the morning. I was having a few bad dreams myself but nothing nightmarish enough to remember.

They leave the light on all night in each unit. They do turn them off inside each cell but the unit light is so bright the effect only approximates dimness. It is comfortable to read by if you can't sleep, but dark enough not to prove a distraction once your eyes are closed. If you want your lights dimmed you can press the intercom button and ask. There's one in each cell and one near the unit door.

I try calling my lover a second time fifteen minutes after the first. No answer. The mechanized operator suggests I try again after four rings. Before I can call him again I'm summoned to the laundry room. It's just as well. Perhaps this brief separation will be good for us. Sometimes I think we're too subsumed in each other. He gets into snits where he can't get enough sex. And once in awhile I get into a like snit. The day before I left we went at it for two hours, couch to floor to bed. I got off twice. He was too tired to get his but remained erect for the whole ordeal. I appreciated his stamina. Maybe that's our trouble, insufficient control over our fleshly appetites. I've long been aware that the business of our lives suffers because of this and we get into trouble—especially me. I end up getting behind in my commitments. I find myself overextended then frantic. I nut up and numb out, unable to do anything but watch movie after movie.

Thinking these thoughts causes me to anticipate my release and return home. Ours should be a very intense reunion, provided he doesn't cheat or masturbate, although it is probably healthier for me to rid my mind of carnal thoughts as long as I'm here. I am convinced that I should regard this period in my life as something spiritual. Like nunhood.

When they clocked me in they asked me if I smoked and I said no. But that last night I put five nails into my coffin to the tune of two large mugs of java. I ran the fan to clear out the smoke and emptied the ashtray and washed it. I didn't want my lover to know how wired I was. The effort was futile; I couldn't hide it. The skin on the back of my hands erupted in nervous dermatitis.

It's now mid-afternoon and I'm called out of my cell to clear a basement room of giant packing crates. I think I'm going to have help but the two White male officers unlock the door and then promptly disappear, leaving me to my own resources, once I'm shown where the dumpsters are located outside the loading dock. I have to lug the monsters, one, two, and three at a time to the elevator and up one floor. On my second trip, Deputy Jane tells me that my lover called. I'm desperate to talk to him, but she warns me that if I take a break it might make the Lieutenant angry. On my first trip, I noticed a bank of pay phones just off the elevator in the corridor leading to the lobby.

I don't have any coins so I use my calling card number. I know it by heart. Our line is busy. I dial zero to get the operator and ask her to put through an emergency call. She cautions me that it will cost me quite a bit more than the average call. I tell her money is no object. It takes a couple of anxious moments but he finally answers.

He was sweating another disaster and didn't want to talk. He was the victim of a hit-and-run. He was plowed into by a mini-van on his way home from work. The van slammed our sedan in the rear door on the driver's side. A Latino in a Dodger-blue cap was at the wheel– had been trying to bogart through the gridlock to cross the boulevard. My lover had been cruising down the empty third lane on the extreme right, passing everyone else, trying to make the light. As he reached the intersection he turned to see the mini-van coming at him on his left. He hit the accelerator and managed to shoot forward enough to avoid personal injury. As he backed up, the other cars parted to let the van driver escape. The bad guy careened through a service station lot and fled in the oncoming rush hour traffic as my man got out to see what the damages were.

No one volunteered as a witness. No one came up with a license plate number. Maybe because he's so big and Black they figured he could take care of anything himself. That's usually the way it goes. Or maybe they just wanted to get where they were going. Or maybe they figured he deserved what he got. He's angry about the whole ugly affair. If he had've been White, he feels, someone would've stopped and played the good Samaritan. I had wanted to talk sweetly of sweet things. I don't argue with him, I try to calm him down.

He's upset because the left passenger door is mangled and the front tires were simultaneously split by impact with the curb, right down to the steel belting. He can drive on them but not for long, and at con-siderable risk; this coming at a time when my case and attorney fees have not only eaten up all our cash but plunged us into the deep red. He riles against this town. It's getting impossible to drive, especially in Hollywood. Drive in any direction for fifteen minutes and you'll avoid one accident per minute.

This accident means he'll have to tough it out awhile in the old struggle buggy. It can only be safely driven at speeds less than forty miles per hour, spews big gusts of pollution, and has sported used tires with paper-thin tread for over two years. I reassure him that once I'm free I'll get a job and we'll soon resume our former rung in the lower middleclass. He tells me that I shouldn't worry, that somehow he'll cope. We tell each other we love us and hang up.

I go back to wrestling with the crates trying not to hurt my back. I manage to scrape a few knuckles on the stucco post of the loading dock. I'm a good worker and it only takes me a half-hour to get the rest of the job done. I go back to jail and head directly to the laundry room where I fold up the last load, the blankets. Fabric softener is used in the wash but it doesn't make a dent in the cotton fiber that feels more like steel wool. I take an additional top sheet back to my cell to protect my delicate skin from the ravages of the vicious gray blanket waiting for me.

I'm the only regular occupant in Unit E. I keep wondering what I'm going to do when I get out of here. When I go for some jobs they're going to ask me about my arrest record. I've already got enough strikes against me, my height, the way I wear my hair, my don't-fuck-with-me attitude, not to mention skin color or thick Negroid features.

It was funny the way the bruthuhs looked at me when they saw me serving lunch. There are six inmates. Five are Black and one's a Mexican–American. The count is likely to increase with the weekend. They probably think I'm here for prostitution. That's always the first guess. Assault comes second because I'm certainly big enough to lay a son-of-a-bitch to rest. The only theft I've ever committed is to rob an employer of time on the job. I'm guilty of doing my best and failing at it. I'm guilty of wanting things I can't afford, of not being satisfied with the way I'm forced to subsist. I feel no remorse. None at all.

Why I'm here is nobody's effin' business. I'm doing light time compared to what I could be doing. Lucky me.

In an hour and a half it'll be dinnertime. I guess they'll call me if they want me to do that. My feet hurt. I take off my brogans but leave my socks on because the cement floor retains the cold. In spite of the discomfort, all this housework makes the time pass quickly, although I'm afraid it's not going to help heal the rash on my hands.

I'd like to call home again, but lover man said he wouldn't be back for awhile, until after six. I don't know where he's gone or why. I try not to let distrust enter my mind. He just couldn't mess with another woman while I'm cooling my derriere in here. That would be too low down. But as I've been told, not everyone can wait. And he's made those kinds of noises before. I'll try to call him again in an hour. I wonder if they monitor the calls? I'd like to feel free to discuss our relationship uncensored. I think of hearing him tell me he loves me over and over again, giving me the reassurance he knows I need. This is my fantasy.

I look at my watch and notice it's time for the evening news. Ah, TV. I get up and turn it on. I discover there's something wrong with it. I can only get two channels, neither worth the effort. I turn it off. Later, Officer Debbie comes on shift, sees me sitting here staring at the walls, opens the door, and asks me, why don't I watch some television? I explain that it only gets two channels. She tells me it's on the fritz and shows me how to adjust the buttons to bring in other channels. Now I discover I can even get the music commercial station. Saved. It's rare that I get to hear the stuff I grew up on or listen to at home, but any kind of music is better than none.

I rarely get to watch this much TV at home without interruptions from the telephone, neighbors, or my lover wanting to watch "the game." The sitcoms I hated are tolerable when there's nothing else to watch. I'm able to get the ice skating championships regularly. I'm watching them just now. I enjoy them as never before. When a skater glides across the ice, I find myself gliding with them, to my left and to my right, enthralled as a strange hunger seizes me. I envy their grace, lightness, and agility. It's as close to flying as humans come. When they do a spectacular jump or spin, I whistle and stomp my feet like I'm watching a title fight. Funny. I never cared about this sport before. I never watched it at home. The only time I ever saw people ice skating in reality I thought it was silly. There were no Black skaters then, and most things White people enjoyed that excluded us seemed silly.

Suddenly I'm aware that eyes are on me. I look up.

Immigration is in. They're marching twenty-odd young Mexicans by my unit. Mestizos. The men are getting a kick out of waving at me and blowing kisses through the glass. They're all unkempt, beige skin browned further by the sweat and grit of their aborted journey north. None of them are bigger than a minute and most in their late teens and early twenties. They make me laugh. Three young Mestizas bring up the rear and peer in at me to see what the commotion was all about. One is very pregnant. I guess I'll be preparing them breakfast depending on how fast they're processed out of here.

By Friday the count doubles, and by Monday morning it will have tripled if not reached capacity. So far thirty-two Chicanos have been rounded up and slapped in the hoosegow. A few are older men who hold their heads down and seem ashamed of their situations. They keep their shirts on. The others, beautiful young *vatos,* sport tattoos on chests and extremities, everything from simple names like Nila, Paula, Tamara, Gloria, and *mia Madre* to intricate weavings of Madonna-and-Child, daggers, crosses, serpents, and the signatures of turfdom-like 102nd Street. One is an Asian mix and one is a Black mix. I'm as tall or taller than all of them. *Poquito lindos.* They all say "thank you" in English when I hand them their suppers. The homegrown guys don't say shit.

It appears I'll remain alone in this unit. All the other women in the world are out there being law-abiding housefraus, computer programmers, and stenos. Actually I have a roomy, but she doesn't speak. She's a part-timer on work furlough. She's the exact physical counterpart of Deputy Jane, a blonde banty-woman. I call her Sleeping Booty. She's supposed to help out in the kitchen but she swoops in, spends about fifteen minutes putting the peaches into cups and then splits, leaving me to do the rest.

During the afternoons it gets cold in my bunk, like the inside of the fridge. I guess they turn off the air-conditioning at some point during the night, or turn it down, because it gets awfully warm in here and I can hardly breathe which further complicates the process of sleep. When I get up in the morning I feel overcooked. Even a cold shower doesn't help. When I get to the kitchen I go into the freezer for a couple of minutes. That and three cups of cold lemonade usually helps. By late morning I'm ready for a cup of coffee. God, I could use something stronger.

The air-conditioning dries out my already dry skin. I keep layering on lotion. It doesn't help the dermatitis at all, and the skin at the site of irritation is tender and red from repeated dippings into dishwater. This jumpsuit is made for a woman with a shorter torso and is too snug in the crotch. It chafes when I raise my hands above my head. By late evening I'm rubbed unpleasantly raw. All this bodily itchiness contributes to later sleeplessness.

Sleeping on the futon leaves me restless. It always takes awhile for me to doze off. The next morning I feel bruised to the bones. The cement floor seems softer. I scoot down and sit on it when I'm on the phone.

My dreams are fragmented and when I wake I feel deprived. Like some important message has been lost. Once I fell asleep for a couple of hours after lunch. I dreamed I missed a visit from my lover. In my dream I had lain down for a nap and couldn't rouse myself even though I heard them calling my name over and over again on the intercom. My body trembled but my eyes refused to open.

I've been a daydreamer since childhood so escaping boredom has seldom been problematic. I'm always fascinated with myself. Now I guess I'll have plenty of time to do some deep exploration; the kind of time I never have at home. If I put my mind to it I might come up with some moneymaking scheme or map out some plan to make major changes in my life. I have googobs of meditation time. With some intense concentration I can probably recreate some of the best nights of my life, or at least occupy myself by trying. And in no time I'll be out of here, and all this will be a dream if not a vaguely disturbing memory. When I'm liberated, I can try and do something about those dreams.

The fact is, in here it's mighty hard to shake off the dreamlike quality of day-to-day existence. It is minimal and unreal. This realization is complicated by my knowledge of life outside because there is very little difference between being inside and outside. Except that if I don't work a job every day I understand that I will suffer some very dire consequences on the outside. There is no such suffering in here. There is almost nothing I can do to either better or worsen my condition, given my state of mind and character.

Inside, everything that was outside seems better, although my good sense tells me it wasn't.

Like loving my man.

I am lonely now. But I was lonely before—in his company. How can that be?

We kissed, touched, made love.

But looking back on it, imagining it—his eyes, the feel of his lips brushing mine, the strength in his hands and thighs—all better now, more vivid than when I was having the experience.

In here we never argue.

In here, everything that didn't work out there is suddenly workable. The solutions that eluded me are suddenly clear. Why? Now I know what it was I needed to do to make this or the other thing happen. I see how to make the right moves, in lieu of the wrong moves made in the recent past. I know exactly what I'm going to do when I get out. I know how I'm going to shake things up. I know that I'm not going to ever have one wasted minute again. Is this some kind of mental trick I'm playing on myself? A phenomenon common to the incarcerated that I know nothing about but am experiencing nevertheless?

The longer I'm here, the more I rely on the music. Listening to the lyrics, when they come, has become a distinct pleasure. I have the patience to memorize them, now. And to trip with the music. Fortunately, most of it is rock and roll and not that horrible watered-down stuff or classical. I go to that place in time the music takes me. I go there and linger in the minutes before sleep. Singing myself a silent lullaby of the sounds I like to hear.

This is my life now, for this moment—the distant faces of authorities and inmates, the kitchen, the TV, the music. It is terrible in its simplicity, weighty in its ease and regimentation.

The dreams of my lover are the best dreams of all. I have as much of his attention as I crave, in the way I crave it.

I am as happy here as I was out there.

Oddly.

And *that* is what bedevils me.

Shark Liver Oil

FOLLOW ME, Jack or Jill—if you will. You know, in Chinese lore, white is the color of death and corruption. 'Tain't necessarily so, like the Man sings in the Song. *Howsumevah*, kick back and allow me to hip you to my color-whacked past ... then you tell moi ...

Hear that low distant rumble? That's a plane overhead clearing for landing at Los Angeles International Airport, predominantly Black-owned homes in the crash path. When the eyes adjust to this particular darkness, the center of this universe is a pinprick of light. Follow along as it novas outward to a huge circular enlargement. What appears within the circle is a photograph on torn newsprint. A dark hand grips an object in black-and-white. Blow it up in the mind's eye and zero in on those tense digits. They hug a rifle. That infamous shot of Brother Huey P. Newton, brainiac-in-chief of the Black Panther Party, holding down that wicker chair, hangs by a tack on my bedroom wall.

But let's give credit where credits are due. Whammer-jammered in, like rivets—soundlessly staccato. Like bullets from a silencer—a splash of Peter Max from the hind of the psychedelic '60s. We take it slow and dissolve into a cruise—say, forty-five miles per hour. When the light hits another photograph, just the two of us raised-fisted rakes in black berets and wigs *au naturel*, all that proud kinky-wavy overflow, sporting black leather jackets dressed up for the get-down, impersonating the liberated. We are cousins raised as brothers. I'm Gregory Joseph and he's Dennis Ray. No surnames just now, if ever. They tagged me Jeeter because of the noise my teeth made when, as a child, I caught cold. Him we call D-Ray.

Reverse the positive and freeze.

City livin's all *roman noir*. The cow town of our birth is no exception and has appropriated the phrase. This is not the text our hearts have written. We are far from being in control. No, the author of this madness wrote the bestseller and cackled all the way to the bank before we were even the wiggle on a sperm.

Listen to our theme music. It's the national anthem. It accompanies our scenario on urban racism circa the post-JFK days of the late twentieth century. It segues into a soulful sister balefully accompanying herself on piano, singing softly and plainly, "Man—where are you now that I need you?"

But right now, everything is jake.

It is 1967 and we are ace boon coons barely out of our teens rolling with the Black Knights Community Alert Patrol. We go by assumed names to protect our kin. We don't know it yet, but we will fail because who we are is not nearly as politically astute as "they" imagine—yet "they" have sent their stooges to infiltrate us, those paid informants who squeal in the dark, Black like us but guys-on-arranged-release who are blackmailed or extorted into the snitch, as well as undercover Negroes who swing both ways—as infiltrators and agents provocateurs.

But they are not half as effective as that scourge of the Los Angeles Police Department known as the 111th Street Division. It is us against them. What we are about is payback for the crimes these so-called servants of the law continue to commit against us and those who sympathize with us.

On the evening in question D-Ray and me have spied and are trailing this undercover plainclothes muthafuckin' pig of a cop.

Among his street evils, he deals dope and sells firearms to teens. We do not know it now, but we are driving into a setup that will alter life as we struggle through it. We will be seen, if not recognized, and traced. We will flee the City of the Angels for distant climes. The false accusations against us will undermine the very organization to which we've sworn allegiance.

Meanwhile, back at the plantation . . . the leaders-and-spokesmen of our organization are liquored up and making the rounds, being professionally vocal and espousing the Cause as talk-show fodder of the era. Today our peoples are on radio miking it down to some master clown whose alias is Sam "the Spam" Sycamore. We have tuned in, kicked back, and are listening to the agony of words being twisted and ideas trashed. Sam waxes smoothly.

". . . our sponsors thank you, I thank you. This is, indeed, *The Sam Sycamore Show* . . . where we chop issues down-to-size . . . and the people who need it! Our guests today . . . we'll go to the phones later and allow you, the listening public, to put in your two cents . . . but first on tap are four members of the Black Knights . . . including their spokesman—"

"Sorry to interrupt you, Brutha Spam, but we's *all four* spokesmen!"

"Donald Tarrigan. The voice you just heard belongs to Mr. Tarrigan . . ."

"Spelled with two r's-uh huh!"

". . . who is here with three of his lieutenants, Conrad Jeffries, one-ah, gentleman—who prefers to be known as Dragon and—I'm sorry what did you say?"

"Wrong on that Jeffries. The name's Conrad X, man! Conrad X! Get the moniker straight, Lame."

". . . extraordinary, yes, Comrade X . . . and finally a guest known by his *nom de guerre* as Raven! Now, let's address the reason for your presence here . . . some say your Police Monitor Cadre is nothing but a bunch of vigilantes intended to antagonize public servants . . ."

"Nonono! We're addressing a clear and present need in our community to protect Black men, women, and children who are constantly molested by unscrupulous officers of the law."

"Damned straight!" D-Ray and me chime in on that one, even though no one can hear us. We are parked curbside, waiting for the pig we're following to come out of the liquor store.

"Like Brutha Tarrigan say, we tired . . . tired of pig poleece comin' 'round an' beatin' on peoples, shootin' . . . treatin' us like dirt . . . like we was . . . animals!"

"But is it fair for you to *claim* that all police are guilty of misconduct?"

"Claim! Was Jesse James an outlaw?"

"Did the Titanic sink?"

"We knows those pig suckas feel free to do whatever they please because there's no repercussions and no justice for those who complain."

"Mister . . . er . . . Raven, do you agree?"

"I must. I'm with them. Brutha Tarrigan speaks the gospel."

"And just how long do you intend to scrutinize L.A.'s Finest as they go about their duty of protecting law-abiding citizens?"

"We'll be on them like lice onna' dog . . ."

"Grease onna' pig . . ."

The laughter is ours.

"Mind you, we're not just watching the police, but the Sheriff and his deputies—even the U.S. Marshal—anyone who dares terrorize our community," Dragon pipes.

When the show is over we are concerned about the easy rhetoric and obvious grandstanding. The name of the game is goad, incite and pander. We know that everyone has been entertained, but we were hoping the consciousness of that other community across town might be raised. Phone calls from the public underscore the foolishness of such a naive hope. That wasn't what Sam "the Spam" was about anyway.

Now, my mind wanders those wide poorly kept streets that comprise our turf—South Central. It is a cool late December afternoon. When I look closely, I again admire the sleek lines of that maintained black-and-tan 1958 Pontiac. I can hear the funk bumpin' mellow through the neighborhood. Our quarry exits the LIQ. We watch. He and his bunky climb into an unmarked Dodge maria and cruise past. We've ducked down under the dashboard. It is obvious, to we two young bloods laying dead behind the wheel, that the pigs are on the grunt. We rev the Pontiac and follow, cautiously.

Getting in tight from the rear, anyone could get a strong whiff of pomade and sweat. As I recall, we are readers. Our love affair with danger began with Willard Motley's *Knock On Any Door* and *Let No*

Man Write My Epitaph (the title alone gave us the high). Malcolm X inspired us purely. Just now, we're chewing on *Down These Mean Streets* by Piri Thomas. You dig? The most literate thugs who ever (all praise to Kali) konked a fool on the head with some bona fide knowledge.

"Right on, D-Ray." I speak with authority. "Maintain the pace. Keep us some distance. Close ... not too close now. Them mutha-fuckin' White boyz are dumb ... but not all dumb. Let 'em look all they want, we lookin' to see what they lookin' at."

"Is this a steering wheel in my hand? I'm drivin' Jeeter. My turn, for real. Why don't you jes be content to ride shotgun and shut the fuck up."

"Man—I rode shotgun twice already, 'member?"

"Just keep that camera ready."

I give Baby a caress. She's a birthday gift from my Uncle James— a quite pricey 16-millimeter with zoom. The pride of the fleet, so to speak. Few can afford anything above Instamatic snaps, 8 mm tops. I imagine myself doin' it at my shoulder like the real deal—shooting the action. Now if we can get some generous soul to blow for the lab fees ...

"They're slowin' up. Destination must damned near be zero."

"Stay smooth, D-Ray, stay smooth."

Now let's get supernatural with it.

Imagine we're the flies on the interior of that unmarked '66 Dodge, bug-eyin' two White men in dark suits and cheap ties. One thinks of starched collars and serious five o'clock shadow. Both are on the burly side but unrumpled. With our antennae to the ether, we discover they're off-duty as of an hour (the police radio is muted, but we hear the buzz from time-to-time). They are known as Detectives Jim O'Sullivan and Eddie Brugh, all of thirty-two—with a bullet—and hard, slack faces.

"Are we set, Brugh? Did Turley buy it?"

"Big time, Jimbo."

"Blab! Why's a guy run off at the mouth, Eddie?"

"Too many brews. Zamagian sez he was tanked, Catholic conscience ... who the hell knows. You're a fuckin' Mick ... you should appreciate it, ex-altar boy qualms or the guilty like."

"Leave the fuckin' Church out of it, Dutchman. Turley thought he grew an extra ball—the mouthy butthole. Me, I was never for him knowin' jack shit. Let alone bein' a player. He's not in our league when it comes to guts."

"Listen up, Tonto. If it'd been anybody in that booth at Massolino's other'n Zee. And Grametti, an' that dumbfuck, Rice—our asses could be dry grass."

"Yeah. An' Turley the prairie fire or the fuckin' match at least."

"This match gets extinguished. Anyway, Grametti thinks Turley might've weaseled to his brother-in-law ... ya' know, Senator Win Meadows?"

"Win'll put a zipper on his own mouth. He knows if he takes people down, he goes with 'em. He's 'Code' all the way. Turley ... he ain't been married ... what was it? Three years? 'Member his bachelor party?"

"He put a front porch on that skinny bitch fast 'enuff." Brugh snorts to clear his ears.

"Kid's better off gettin' introduced to Daddy Warbucks. Too bad."

"An orphan-to-be. I'm fuckin' consumed with grief." Brugh hee-haws like a jackass. "The plant-piece is in that valise in the trunk. Got it filed clean?"

"Naw. It's one of Zamagian's. Took it off some punk-ass bean-eater, couple years back. Probably unregistered. It's from down below the border, so far from home clean don't matter. Zee sez it's made in Spain. Came with a silencer..."

Get the idea fellow flies? Some dirty doings are about to go down. And here we are playing Super Snoop and Double-O-Soul, serenaded by more Motown sound than our itchy feet can dance.

"'S gettin' dark, D-Ray. This camera ain't gon' be much use."

"Whatever plays with them muthafuckas plays."

"One of those dudes in that Dodge tried to bust my ass for shop-liftin' a couple of years back."

"No jive. How'd you beat that rap?"

"Full alibi. Coincidentally, it was that liquor store on the corner, where my Aunt Mable lives. My cuz Horace works there. He told 'em it wasn't me because it wasn't. Another witness backed him up."

"Bailed out yo' luck-a-fied black ass..." I snorted. D-Ray was blessed.

"She-it. Rub my head, muthafucka."

We laugh loud and long. Then D-Ray is seized by a sad irony. "My cuz Willie thought he was the lucky one. Always coppin' stuff and gettin' away clean. And then one time he got caught. He got offered the alternative of military service. My boy bragged until he hurt my feelings, you know? I bet he'd like to be up in San Quentin servin' time right now."

"How so?"

"At least, then, he'd be in one piece. 'Stead, he got sent straight to Nam. Got both legs blown off."

"Damn."

"Got that right!" But D-Ray is noticing something else that rattles our nerves. Suddenly, there is no other traffic. "Jeeter, this is junkass territory. Don't dig this, Homes." He eases up off the accelerator and taps the brakes. We slow to a crawl putting distance between us and the unmarked Dodge. The area is run-down and industrial. We cross old railroad tracks and enter a concentration of weathered deserted buildings, warehouses with broken windows—a slum within a slum. Not a soul in sight.

"Pssst—Jeeter, they parkin'!"

"Down this street! Turn, fool! Curb it! Anything!"

Our heads jerk side-to-side in the panic. D-Ray makes a lurching stop against the curb and we bounce for a minute. I switch off the radio. We're on a grimy, small street that has that dead-end feel. We instinctively know we are on the edge. It rattles us. D-Ray kills the motor, snatches a look in the rear-view mirror. I look over my shoulder. We are following them, yet we feel trapped.

"Is this a trick? You don't think those cops deliberately let us follow them, do you?"

"This is the kind of setup where people get shot for resistin' arrest." I imagine us on our knees, cuffed from behind.

"Or—'Two Unidentified Splibs Found Slain in Gangland Killing.' She-it." D-Ray is more of a cynic than I am, be that possible.

There's no obvious escape route that we can detect. To our left is a cracked paved alley in the process of reverting to woods. It's cloudy, threatening rain, and the weather is driving a darkening of our psyches, a visceral animal thing. Until this moment, we were having fun monitoring the Pig. It was like manful boasting around the campfire about the grizzly hunt, passing the joy juice like back in the days of mountain men or railyard scab laborers. Without thinking that maybe behind that bush, an angry grizzly or union boss lurks—that perhaps we are the hunted.

Our freeze status is broken before either can speak. Lights momentarily splash the interior, and we duck under the dash long enough for the second vehicle to pass. Boldly, D-Ray sneaks a peek.

"She-it," he whispers. "Now we got two unmarked cop cars. Looks like a genuine lynch party."

Zamagian and Turley are undercover cops off duty. This is their Tuesday night "offline" party. Beer, gin, rye, confiscated grass, and the loud talk of bulls. Turley has no reason to suspect this is anything but back slaps, war stories, wife, and mother-in-law jokes. The usual get shit-faced puking-drunk knowing-you've-been-rotated-out-for-two-days copfest. He's not made his will.

Turley's only thirty-six, an ex-high school/junior college flunked-out football player, pumped up on iron but going-to-fat, thick-necked and heavy-thighed, somber and mean. He has less than fifteen minutes to live but doesn't know it.

It's getting chilly, but me and D-Ray are sweatin' bullets. Nevertheless, D-Ray gives off a resolve I sense without seeing.

My heart beats faster.

"D-Ray, what the hell they doin'? Who they gonna bust way out here? I'm thinkin' maybe we should split. It'll be dark soon, anyhow."

"Maybe Narco set up a buy and Homicide is in on it. Anybody down 'round here is liable to be from the 'hood. Let's tip up on them and see. We don't need a camera to be eyewitnesses."

"Don't you mean dead dogs?"

"Don't pussy out on me, Jeeter. They could be doing something illegal themselves and may not suspect they're being followed. Let's check it out. If so—we could be heroes."

"If we live to tell about it."

"Yeah. They could be baitin' us, lurin' us. It's a chance I'm willin' to take to get even-steven with that asshole Brugh."

"Okay, D-Ray. Deal. But if we get killed I'm on your behind for the rest of eternity."

"Walk sideways."

D-Ray cracks his door and slides to the ground, walking on his haunches. "You coming?"

My better judgment disappears in his urgent whisper and I do likewise, the door resting against the latch, not fully closed. We move rapidly up that bleak street, in and around giant canisters and dumpsters, with the stealth of foot soldiers. It is one hell of a rush. We are concealed in the shadows with full view of the street, the residue from distant street lamps faintly illuminating the vehicles in question. Suddenly D-Ray stops and clutches at me, pulls me close and damn near bites my ear off.

"There's a third unmarked cop car up there in a spot off that lot across the way."

"Where'd that come from?"

"I don't know. But there ain't a pig in sight. If there's another way in here there's another way out."

We're about to find out that the car in question belongs to Chief Steve "Steverino" Grametti. By now it is obvious we are not their intended victims, we think. But there is little point in volunteering. Our heads rotate toward one another. Soundlessly, D-Ray points, jabs the night air with his finger. I bob my head to let him know I'm alert and ready. We slide close enough to see and be seen. I misread his signal and bump him again.

"Damn, Jeeter. I said wait."

"Where'd they go?"

"They gotta be up the street. Let's check 'em out."

We find another alley. It bisects another, small, potholed street, more of an alley itself. We skitter across. A bit further down looms the rear of a destroyed warehouse. The metal is rusted, the concrete is cracked, the mortar crumbling. There are huge holes in the rear wall where the lumber has splintered and rotted away. A truck might have torn out a hole like that, backing into it, or some loading cart out-of-control. A door is hanging sidewise, held by rusty bottom bolts beneath broken rear windows.

The future we might have had as lawmakers, fighting for our people's cause, flashes before me. The truth is, I love books more than politics. And I'm starting to regret turning down that scholarship I was offered to Pepperdine University. D-Ray is no lightweight either, even if he did drop out after that bullshit altercation with Coach Sting, which didn't make sense to anyone. D-Ray was the best quarterback on the team...

The distant but distinct sound of voices interrupts my thoughts— more mutter than speech. We've reached the edge of that door hanging from its bolt. D-Ray crouches slightly and peers through the broken wall. I'm breathing down his neck. We make out what must have been the office space of some sort of manufacturing plant. There's a battered desk and old paint-flaked file cabinets. A smudged tote-board map is affixed to one office wall—there's a large blackboard effect without the black. Two worn benches, a stool, and a couple of three-legged chairs are flung aside. There's an old water cooler, the glass upper portion shattered. A grim light spills down from cracked panes in a large sky-light above.

We freeze when the voices stop, like they've heard something, are alerted, and now listening. Fear trickles down the back of my jacket neck, wetting my T-shirt. I'm no coward, but I'm not anxious to go out a humbug in this rat-infested ramshackle monument to American know-how. D-Ray is fearlessly driven by his vendetta. To my relief the voices start up again, and careful-footed, we advance toward them. There's a breezeway blow of soft sound, a cough, some skitter-scratch of footfalls, a burp, a throat clearing, some muffled short conversation. The sound of my heartbeat is so loud it's a wonder I hear anything.

D-Ray freezes again. I lean into him and peer over his shoulder. Before us there's an up-ended desk, a cylinder-like assemblage the size of a tree trunk, some iron rods and fallen aluminum siding. Dangerously noisy doings are ahead. D-Ray grabs my shoulder and points. To our right there's a ladder affixed to the wall. It doesn't go far, about fifteen feet to a small loft. A storage shed, observation booth, or some kind of makeshift file room is up there. The raised office has stairs, a partially standing stairwell. We mount and scale it. From a roughly southeast angle, the new elevation discloses the entire main floor below. Bingo. We count five plainclothed pigs. Oink for days.

Fragments of speech drift up. We crouch low, crawl along the railing and check the scene as it plays down. Someone's brought a lamp which gives up just enough light for us sneaky petes to match each voice to a man, portions of bodies, fractions of faces revealed.

". . . fuckin' broad down in Chinatown . . . I sez yeah, I eat Chinese." Brugh is apparently spinning some kind of dirty yarn. "Wrapped up Thursday. The dumb sonuffabitch decked 'em." But it makes little sense to us—at first.

"Transferred, yeah. The butthole went to Palo Alto. Bobby sez he's goin' to night school. . ." The one they call Zamagian caps it off.

"Ha! Ha! Ha!" Now the bunch of 'em is breaking their faces, slapping knees and backs. A loose thread is picked up.

"The highrollin' fucker was wearing the maid's dress while she was back with her taco-scarfin' relatives . . . *hermosilla* . . . offed himself. Yeah. The old dame found him in lipstick, high heels, dressed-to-the-hilt comin' out party—GOIN' OUT, HA!" Brugh is on a howl, his sides splitting.

"Blowed half his face off. . . fuckin' nosey nigger born a pimp came out of the womb pimpin' his ol' lady. Wants to get all them niggers on welfare. Put the gun right behind his ear, his ear to the wall . . . to the wall!" O'Sullivan chimes in on the horror story. D-Ray and I exchange a terrible look. These are some stomp-down death angels.

"I sez, hey kike, your fuckin' Big-Shit Uni-ver-sit-ty law degree don't mean shit to me . . . brown-nosin' more like it . . . suckin' up to every pimple-faced jerkoff in the D. A.'s office." Zamagian adds another ugly two cents.

There's a sudden flash the size of a roach going up. Turley's lit a cigarette with his lighter. A half-pint of hooch makes the rounds. Zamagian is poppin' another six-pack and passing the brew. These pigs are definitely having a party, looks like. Chief Grametti points a finger. There's something thick and white riding it.

"Mess up your lungs, Turley. Use some good shit."

Our eyes bug out. The Chief himself has lit a marijuana cigarette and is taking deep tokes, a joint damned near big as a cigar. The smoke wafts up our way and we fight ourselves silly, trying not to betray our whereabouts at this unexpected turn.

"Yeah. You could get to be a heavy-ass hippie like the Chief." Brugh laughs so hard he coughs.

"Stuff makes me too sleepy . . . horny 'n' hungry," Turley chuckles back, but we see he doesn't think it's so ha-ha funny.

"Suppose to . . . make you relax. You've been a little jumpy lately, Turley." Brugh's got the joint now and is blimping.

"Don't cuff the joint, Brugh. I'm the one needs relaxin'. My kid's cuttin' teeth." Zamagian reaches for it.

"Haaahaa—fuckin' Zee can't get his zees!" The Chief is into word-play to boot. Me and D-Ray's sides are splitting from holding in our shock, surprise, and laughter. They've been busting and rousting nig-gahs so long they've even learned to talk our talk. And sassy with it. We could like these closet goons if they weren't so inhuman when it comes to non-White folk.

"That's a trip, Zamagian—you fuckin' *turkey*. Stop humpin' your ol' lady, get her tubes tied, get yourself fixed." Turley takes a swig of hooch.

"Hey, hey! Turley, you know better'n to ever mention a Turk to an Armenian. You walkin' a thin wire, bud, with no balancing pole." Zamagian takes the joint again, washes the smoke back with brew. "Whoooo this shit is quality. I'm startin' to level off. They lent me out to Hollenbeck station . . . you know that headless dame in that Boyle Heights garage? Had to clean up after that psycho. Talk about wired? I'm like a cat with his tail skinned."

"Talkin' of tail, you gettin' any Officer Turley? Dipped the wick lately?"

D-Ray went into something akin to an epileptic fit. I grabbed him and put my fingers to his lips. Under Brugh's humor, I hear some-thing scary.

"Me and Sims picked up a couple of beaner hookers out near Union Station last week." But Turley doesn't suspect a thing, cracks a beer can. "Sprinkled some salsa on those *putaritos*."

"My, my, you been down right sinful, Turley." O'Sullivan had been

84

mighty quiet, nursing his beer like a grudge. And while I can't see it, I imagine an evil glint in his eye.

"*Mea culpa*, Father Jimmy." Turley must've smirked. He isn't takin' any shit, serious or otherwise.

"Gotta flippant attitude Turley, badmouthin' the Church." O'Sullivan coils up like a cobra in the sudden ominous silence. Brugh stretches and looks up in our direction. We freeze, except for my stomach which flips over so loudly it's a miracle they don't hear it down there. Then his eyes fasten on Chief Grametti who leaves the loop, staggers toward a dim wall near some debris and takes a p-stance, groaning "ahhh" as he relieves himself. This time me and D-Ray go into spasms of unspent laughter.

"Drain that radiator, Chief. Hose it down!" Zamagian cracks.

"That's the fuel tank, you fuckin' Armenian geek. You pussies think goddamn beer's a man's drink. You got no class. A real man needs his liquor hard." Chief Grametti zips his fly and wrestles with his belt buckle. "Damn cheapass..."

"What's a shithead wop know about anything that ain't vino?" Zamagian snipes and everybody roars. These fools like the smell of their own squat.

"Zee, you just wanta get in my pants, ya fag. That's why you say shithead so polite. I'm savin' my cherry for a choice piece of police cunt... like Angie whats-her-name in Narcotics. She can sit on my face anytime." Grametti chokes a taste and wipes snot with the back of his hand.

"Busta your balls, Dago. She'd probably cuff you to the bed... chew off your itty-bitty nuts. You still takin' those jig whores off interrogation in the back seat 'round here?" Brugh gives us cold chills as we imagine these pigs brutalizing our womenfolk.

"Keep stickin' that dipstick inta that nasty chute and it'll be fallin' off soon. Probably got the siff now—it'll affect your mind soon." Turley spat a laugh.

"Lose it! O'Sullivan, did he ever have it? Hey, ain't no coon cunt gonna faze my man. More likely, he'll wind up on skid row, old fart, pissin' his pants in a bunk at the Midnight Mission." Zamagian smirks as he hands Grametti a beer.

"Fuck you, Zee. Plyin' me with this swill, eh? Brugh, anymore reefer? While the rest of you—especially you Zamagian—are still cruisin' the jackoff booths an' bath houses goin' down on all them queers, I'll be on my yacht, anchored off Catalina, or Honolulu, or maybe I'll retire-with-the-royalty."

"Royalty? Grametti—you're a royal pain in the butt. Left me stranded at third, that softball game last year 'gainst those dickheads from Foothill Division. Couldn't even manage a fly ball to the outfield."

It dawns on D-Ray and me that we are tuned to the drunken ravings of a pig brotherhood, ragging and bragging, a treasured tradition of the universal fraternity of men with a common bond—one we've practiced ourselves. But these are the nastiest muthafuckas we've ever encountered.

"Takes one to know one. Grametti is a natural switchhitter, an' he's battin' from his weak side." Brugh laughs.

"Any side this side of money's a weak side. But he's a switch-hitter all right." Zamagian empties another can, throws it away. "He's always checkin' crotch for weapons and every fat-assed whore we shake down for peddlin' her gash. Retire! Hell, Grametti, you retired ten seconds after you graduated the academy."

"At least I graduated. If you didn't suck me off every morning you'd be on the corner your damned self." Grametti makes like he's going to throw that can at Zamagian. He crushes it with one hand and tosses it into the dark.

"He's got a jones for crawlin' up nigger ass." Brugh spits and scratches his groin. D-Ray is silent now, eyes zeroed in on Brugh like radar. He wishes he could reduce this particular pig to ashes.

"Shit! That he does, and how! Well, I'm ready for the rockin' chair, boys. A fat-ass fuckin' retirement pension!"

"Sometimes I wish my retirement wasn't so damned far off." Turley stares at his brew like its bitter. "A man . . . get's tired."

His words seem to set off something in the others. There's a definite change in attitude. We feel it in the air.

"You tired . . . Turley? Ready to ride off inta the sunset? Shit, you ain't paid half the dues the Chief's paid. Right guys?"

"No—I—" Turley's thrown by Brugh. He senses something too.

86

"I think the man is real tired. Maybe he needs a nap-big-time nap. Anyway, I'm about ready to split. Party's over."

"So, Turley . . . life's a bitch? Why don't we all take an early retirement?" Brugh's wild-eyed.

"Hey! Fellas? Why so serious all of a sudden?" Turley drops the can to his feet and kicks it.

D-Ray taps my hand and points.

O'Sullivan is stepping away from the group, slides to one side. He lifts up his sport coat, which lies atop a small black valise, runs the zipper, his back to them, and quickly draws a glove over his shooting hand then lifts and hefts this ugly weapon, screws on the silencer, turns and steps back into the group. They've all gotten quiet now. And they're all staring at Turley.

"See, Turley, life's like an elevator. . ." Brugh nods at O'Sullivan. "For some people it goes up, slow or fast. For others it goes down."

Zamagian, Grametti, and Brugh slowly edge back. Turley is isolated and senses trouble through his drunk. Turley turns his head slightly, sees O'Sullivan's got the muzzle leveled.

"Whoa! What the fuck! Sully! Hey—what's going on?"

"You're the man of the hour, Turley. You're set to squeal."

"Jezus Christ! Jeezis, Sully! I ain't no rat! Guys—Jeeez!"

"Fuckin' blazzfeemer. Shut up, asshole." O'Sullivan spits.

"Guys! Please . . . stop 'im! Don't do it! Ohhno—my kid—Betty!" Turley's going into a victim's crouch, damned near on his knees.

"Say your prayers, you blubberin' stoolie," Brugh heehaws. "This is what a man gets who informs on his friends."

O'Sullivan squeezes the trigger. There are two muffled whoopfs. Turley goes into a death shimmy.

"Go—od."

He swallows his last word and slumps to a heap, dropped on his knees, head back, startled eyes bugging eternity.

"To the point, if not short," Grametti spits.

Then, too sudden, Brugh raises his arms and points, talking directly at our hiding place. My feet tingle. "Come on down and join the party, you punks. We've saved plenty ammo for your black asses."

Chills course my blood. I'm frozen. D-Ray slaps my shoulder. He points toward the stairwell, then at the loose waffles of the metalloid shed behind us. I follow D-Ray's hand signals. We dart upside the shed and give it a shove. The whole thing strains and collapses, the motion sending the two large rectangles comprising the roof and outermost wall flying over the railing and below. The pigs squawk and scatter. We dash for the stairs, glide down them, and scramble for the exit. I imagine I hear the muffled sounds of bullets whizzing. Our youth favors us as we race through the dilapidated building and jump that hole in the wall and are halfway across the yard before they can say Cassius Clay. I'm running track so hard my stomach's beating my backbone. D-Ray can barely stay on my heels.

"Get the car, Jeeter. You drive!" D-Ray shouts as he tosses me the keys. "Pull up near where Grametti's cruiser's parked. I'll keep 'em busy."

"With what?"

"With this." D-Ray brandishes his stiletto. Perfect for puncturing and slashing the tires on pigmobiles.

"Whowhee!" I holler and crank it up a notch. While D-Ray gets to it, I jump the Pontiac, start it and burn rubber up the block. D-Ray dives in next to Baby. I throw the stick into reverse and back up to where I saw that alley, swerve into its mouth, and dart out again, grateful for the cover of night and a city council too cheap to put adequate lighting in the ghetto.

After our significant getaway, we hold out in the back of Uncle Ducey's Pool Parlor and sort out the madness. We know it will close in soon.

"We can run, but we can't hide from Brugh," D-Ray trembles. "We're their alibi."

"Huh? What's that mean—alibi?"

"Those dirty pig bastards have set us up for that cop killing. They know who we are, Jeeter. Somebody in the Patrol ratted us out. That's why they didn't stop us from followin' them. And if they have anything to say about it, after they put us under the jail—if we're lucky enough to get arrested instead of being killed outright on some trumped up charges—they're gonna fry us for it."

"Damn! Why don't they put all that effort into chasing criminals?

88

We're the good guys. An infiltrator among our ranks?" My stomach was fighting my tongue. "D-Ray—that don't make sense!"

"It does if you've ever stopped to wonder what it would take to bust up the Black Knights Community Alert Patrol. You know how weak our bruthas can be when it's time to throw down. Hate the sight of blood. Get smart."

"If we disappear, they can't bust up the Knights."

"They'll get Tarrigan and everybody concerned—on conspiracy. There'll be a lot of pissin' in pants when that all-White jury turns in a guilty verdict."

"No. Not me. Prison? Never. Tijuana's a three-hour drive."

"Can that. First place they'll look. Be constructive."

"Out of town relatives—Chicago, Wichita, New York."

"Sure. But for how long? Things may not cool down here for months. It may be years before we can get the kind of help that matters. Whatever that is and wherever we find it. Remember ... we've got something on 'em. And who knows, if we're lucky, and if we live long enough, we might get the right people to listen."

We aren't, we do, but they won't.

Don't feel cheated. No one could be more cheated than two youths robbed of their innocence. Sappy fact is, I don't dare tell more without revealing my present whereabouts, swimming undetected in the mainstream of life. The here-and-now is beside the point. There's a past that needs to be dug up and dealt with honestly. We watch the evolution of forensic science with well-licked chops. DNA testing is just the beginning. There are countless similar injustices awaiting the light of irrefutable proof. Ours is but one. Buried in the thirty-year history of the 111th, there's a file an inch deep on the unsolved killing of one officer Ralph Turley, detective, Homicide Division, LAPD. It notes that a warrant was issued for suspects Dennis Ray AKA D-Ray and his accomplice, Gregory Joseph, AKA Jeeter, renegade members of the Black Knights, a subversive paramilitary group disbanded within six months of the slaying. Thus our tale is suspended.

In hiding, we will become strangers to ourselves. James Brown is still screaming. Although most of those dummies he screamed on remain deaf or are long dead. Of the smart-and-still-living, most of those only heard the sound of coins dropping and decided to pick up a few for themselves. (Only in Las Vegas or the recording biz.) Talkin' 'bout the rewards of rhythmic repetitions. But we are not yet among either group. We will take our bullets later—for levity's sake—assassinated by Mr. Gaye and disco fever without the benefit of duct tape.

Nevertheless, tragedy rules. The days D-Ray and me longed to share with our nearest and dearest will become choked with unutterable regrets, our nights doubt-consumed, our dreams twisted with the images of a slaying. Indeed, we, the accused, will go separate ways, riven by the fear that doubles as the price paid for continued, if circumscribed, freedom. Like sharks in the waters off the coast, we keep moving, in the twilight of existence, never stopping, rarely looking back...

My Brain's Too Tired to Think

MRS. JACKSON, we've sat in silence for over five minutes. Perhaps you need additional time to gather your thoughts. Would you like to continue our session or should we reschedule?

Continue. I'm sorry I stopped talkin'. But the mere thought of what I have to say exhausts me. It's so heavy, Dr. Flowers. It's as if my brain is worn to a frazzle.

I haven't heard that expression in years.

My mother always used to say that. Ha!

You find something funny?

No. Not a damned thing. Just the opposite. Tragic. The first "shrink" I went to was some prize niggah shrink—no offense intended. You don't mind my sayin' shrink do you?

No, I do not.

I was so tore down behind all the trouble I'm in, I didn't know what to do. I've been away from the church a long time and I couldn't just jump back into that. I'm not much good at bein' a hypocrite—although I have come to appreciate those who feel they have no place to take their troubles except to the Lord. But I had gotten so desperate, my friend Cane offered to take me to one o' his sharin' group sessions where people stand up and talk out their problems with family or what have you.

What brought that about?

It was EarlRay runnin' off. I was shook real bad. I called my friend Cane and started tellin' him about it. He stopped me and told me about his group and said I could go with him, and he'd introduce me, and I could talk, and they'd listen. It was a nice place, somebody's ranch house—as I recall. It was warm with a high ceiling and all these White people standin' about in flannel shirts and stuff, relaxed. I was still in my suit, since I hadn't long got off work. Cane met me outside, and we walked in together. He's a good friend and was tryin' to support me, but Cane's White too, so he doesn't always see things from a Black perspective.

Meaning?

People do things to you when they look at you. People are animals, and their eyes do animal things. Black folk are hypersensitive to that, more so than most. Maybe because of slavery, being brought over and not understanding the White man's ways, and languages forced us to havta learn how to read looks and vibrations. Maybe it got into our blood and got passed along that way. Whatever or however, it seems a fact if you go by me. Not that that always works, 'specially when there's too much confusion and upsettedness. Then the brain gets tired.

All right. Let's accept that as a fact. Go on with your story.

They were welcoming at first. And I needed someone to welcome me, regardless of skin color. Desperation drove me there in the first place. Cane introduced me and told 'em I was deeply troubled. We were all standin' around this big table with a lamp in the center of it. So their faces were half hidden in shadow. They turned to me with these glowing eyes, and their bodies radiated powerful warmth. It felt good and right. I started to tell them about EarlRay and me. It was my understandin' that others had troubles to voice. I tried to be brief and sum things up, to say everything in a balanced and truthful way, given the state of my brain. But I had hardly said three or four sentences when the warmth vanished and they stopped me cold.

Did you say something to offend them?

I don't know. Cane didn't think so when I asked him later. But the group made it clear to me that they didn't want to hear my story in whatever way I needed to tell it. They cut it off before I could even tell it proper. I thought it was because I was a Black woman and the way I expressed myself was too niggerish, so to speak, for them to handle it. But I couldn't be sure.

Perhaps it wasn't you personally. Perhaps they realized that the depth and seriousness of your problems were beyond the range thought helpful.

Listenin' was supposed to be the help—the only kind of help I was seekin'. All's was needed was thirty minutes or so, to let my sorrow flow.

It sounds as if Cane took you to the wrong people. That particular group had most likely established itself to listen to certain types of introspective problems as opposed to larger social problems. Like those related to the death of a child or parent, the insecurities of college years, the interpersonal identity crises and the like. Your problems with EarlRay were outside their capabilities as a group. Therefore, they quickly concluded there was little point to wasting your valuable time or theirs.

Yeah. Well, then why didn't they just say that then? I got the message and what you say wasn't it. It was strange. They didn't even have to discuss it amongst themselves. To a person, male and female, their eyes went cold and diamond-hard all at once. Like a bunch of lambs turnt into wolves before my eyes. "We're sorry, Mrs. Jackson," the leader said without a blink, "you'll have to stop now." Even Cane noticed, and it made him uptight. They were angry at him for bringin' me there. Like I had done somethin' to them when I opened my mouth—disturbin' their preconceived notions, *whatevah*. Cane got upset and embarrassed. I whispered to him to get me the hell out. We left. He was real apologetic. But I was still in the same place, needin' help. And I was angry at and frustrated by that group of symbiotic jackasses to boot.

You're obviously a bright woman. Your problems seem to stem from being unable to obtain enough money to support your children in the manner you'd prefer. What brought you to me, Ms. Jackson? Given your statements, how can you afford to pay for these treatments?

A year of cabbage soup, oatmeal, and peanut butter and jelly sandwiches while workin' myself half to death around the clock. Savin' the good food for my children, of course, and upkeep for the car. But gettin' my body and brain back to workin' right was worth every bit of sacrifice, I figure.

Check it out.

I was workin' full time for slave drivers yet dead broke, between the outrageous rent I got to pay the landlord and EarlRay findin' and stealin' what little money and valuables I had hid about the house. All the free hotline services this town used to have done dried up from lack of state and federal funding. That meant there was no place to go but to County Health Services. I've dealt with County before. Its services are no better than those in the racist private sector—even if I could afford 'em they probably wouldn't do squat for me. County tends to be staffed by marginal bureaucrats who are too overloaded with casework to help you or incompetents who don't give a damn. Don't make too much difference what color they are, a stooge is a stooge. And the minute you find somebody good, they quit for a better job somewheres.

There doesn't seem to be much wrong with your brain at the moment.

94

'Cuse me?

Therefore, you felt EarlRay's psychologist might be of help.

He was my complexion, Dr. Flowers. At least, I thought, I wouldn't have to deal with the cultural barrier. He had been seein' my husband EarlRay. After EarlRay ran off, I went to him thinkin' he, of all people, could appreciate where I was comin' from, since he had spent so much time talkin' to EarlRay.

I didn't expect total sympathy. But *some* would've seemed normal. I wasn't lyin' to him. I went askin' for help. I thought that being a professional, he would at least listen to what I had to say before makin' harsh judgments. After all, I figured EarlRay would do like his mama always said he did as a teen—run off for two weeks or so, then come back home. I needed his shrink's help for me to decide how to handle things when and if he came back—and if he didn't. To help me decide what to do—how to break my pattern if not EarlRay's. I was very distraught, Dr. Flowers.

How are you now?

On the brink.

Of what?

Doin' sumpthin' I can't undo. If you can imagine.

Yes. I can imagine.

See—I called myself tryin' to be a good wife and doin' everythin' for EarlRay I could, to make it easier for him to be a husband in return.

Admirable, but you were setting yourself up for major disappointment. There's a good deal of give and take in so intimate a relationship as a marriage.

95

I guess. But here I got a husband who's basically grown up a juvenile delinquent. He done spent eight of his twenty-six years in and out of racist state-run institutions. He does time a couple years, manages to stay out a couple of years, gets back in trouble, then gets locked up another couple of years. His mama was the first bitch to put him in jail when he burned up some White man's car and she had to pay for it. Okay?

Now here he comes—swears to me that he wants to be a man. I'm about seein' to it that he gets what he wants, if I love him—I thinks. He said he wanted to go back to school like I was tryin' to do. So I call myself helpin' him go through the process. We looked at the community college catalogue together. I asked him what he wanted to be and what he wanted to take. He's got a knack for fixin' anything that runs. They had lots of courses in electrical engineering. He said he wanted to take that. I even went up to the school with him and helped stand in them block-long lines to get registered. It was fun. We played upsies back and forth like a muthafucka.

Ahem.

Oh. Excuse my French.

I helped him fill out all the paperwork, tellin' him what to put in when he didn't know. Then we found out he could qualify for a government scholarship, a few hundred dollars that he didn't have to pay back. I helped him apply for that. Well, about time for school to start, EarlRay didn't seem much interested. That puzzled me, cuz he had been constantly watchin' the mailbox to see if the check for the government scholarship had come. Guess what?

Your husband took the check and spent it without telling you.

Exactamundo. Frittered it away.

He was going along with your scenario for yourself. The ambition of completing an unfinished education was your dream, not his. He went along with it to please you, half-deluded into thinking he could change his usual behavior. His intentions may have been honorable at first. He might have gone through with it, for your sake. Or it may have been a part of an elaborate emotional con job—as you have apparently concluded. Whatever the case, it appears that when the opportunity arose for him to revert to his old ways, he succumbed.

Right. That weak niggah cashed it and smoked it up with his partners. Then, when I was about to find out about it, he skipped.

Would you like a tissue?

No, thanks.
    You see, I called myself tryin' to make a future with him—I encouraged him to follow what he said was his dream. That was the largest amount of money he had ever had in one lump sum that wasn't a paycheck and didn't have to go on the household bills or food. I think when he saw it he wigged out.

Wigged?

Flipped. You know, as in, flipped his wig.

Ah, yes—I remember that expression. A paternal uncle favored it.
    That's typical behavior in individuals who come from impoverished circumstances, lacking the temperament to understand and handle seemingly large sums of money.

I'd call it childishness. The child in him is very strong. I carried most of the responsibilities myself, as I should've, being divorced and havin' two babies. Then meetin' EarlRay and marryin' him. So I made almost no demands on him in that regard, because I wanted us to always be copacetic. Even so, after awhile he seemed to resent what little I asked. All he wanted to do was eat, sleep, get high, and run them streets.

97

Did you have a prenuptial agreement when you went into this marriage—something in writing as to the responsibilities binding on each partner? The division of finances? Given that your children were by a previous marriage?

Are you jivin'? Who was gonna pay for the attorney? That's for rich women. Or women marryin' rich men. Even if I found some community law center still operatin' what good would it've done me? Poor folk go round doin' shit like that'd never get married. I don't believe in that anyway. Way I was raised, marriage is based on trust. If you love someone you trust 'em. I thought EarlRay loved me. I certainly loved him. It was automatically understood. He'd do his best to be man of the house and I'd continue being a mother to my children while fulfillin' my wifely duties to him. That even included the baby he wanted.

He specifically asked you to have a baby?

Yes. But, like I started to say, when I tried to talk to his shrink about these things the man got extremely hostile toward me. As if I had done sumpthin' wrong to him—like he was my husband steada EarlRay.

Oh?

There's a name for that—that sorta over-identifyin' with sumpthin' goin' on with somebody else?

Yes. It's called transference.

Well he was transferrin' like a muthafucka. Excuse my French.

Feel free to speak as you like, Mrs. Jackson. I'm not a censor.

He was terribly unsympathetic to me. He kept lookin' at his watch. It took way longer than an hour to make that rudenik see that my husband hadn't told him the truth about our relationship. That isn't the

98

first time I've been lied on by a man. But what gets me, is that people —men and women too—will usually take the man's part over the woman's. Or society's part. Most people are quicker to judge a woman as the wrongdoer before they'll think unkindly of a man—'specially if she Black.

That's that old double standard at work. We're still not free of it, even in this supposedly enlightened day and age.

It's a heavy price to pay for being the childbearer.

Mrs. Jackson—you're trembling all over. Can I get you something? Some water or hot tea?

No, thank you. It's just thinkin' about all this. It makes my brain shiver. If only somebody had told me the truth about my husband, I never would have married him. But nobody would tell me. Not a one. I thought that was the job of the authorities. But even they didn't tell me. And they knew his history better than I did. When I think of that parole officer, I could jump across his desk and beat him to death—that smug sonofabitch.

I think I should caution you about expressions of violence, Mrs. Jackson. Either to yourself or others. As a licensed practitioner, I'm obliged to report patients who threaten to do harm to others to the authorities. I'd advise you to measure your words when you're overcome by feelings of aggression.

Ain't that a bitch? The same authorities that put me in the shit will turn around and punish me for being angry about being in the goddamned shit, or for tryin' ta get out of it anyway I can.
    Sorry, Dr. Flowers. But I think my rage is justified. Those authorities didn't give me any warnin'. They let me take that nasty man into my home, knowin' I had two young children and they said nuthin'. Dig—this parole officer had EarlRay's rap sheet right in front of me— and it was nine pages long. And he didn't tell me one effin' word. I can

see that White man now, smilin' to hisself. Now I understand that smile. He knew that lots of damage was about to take place. But it would be happenin' to an unsuspectin' Black woman and her children. So it didn't matter. Our lives, our well-being didn't count in the spectrum of American things. Cuz we considered damned near apes anyway. What did he care what happens to a bunch of apes?

What damage are you referring to?

I—I'm gettin' to that.

Were you alone at any time when you saw the parole officer?

No. EarlRay was sittin' right there with us. But the parole officer had my work and home number. Dr. Flowers—he could've called me and spoken to me confidentially if he had wanted to. He could've warned me if he had wanted to. Don't you see, Dr. Flowers? I was trapped between the racist authorities and a gang of sickos. I had no one to turn to.

This gang you're referring to?

EarlRay's dopehead brothers, his street crimies, and his mother Shurli. She was the ringleader. She was supposed to be my *girlfriend*. I thought a for-real friend. I found out later that not only did she lie about her son, but did not tell me the truth about her own skanky self. Plus my so-called friend Bonnie was in on it—constantly callin' me on the phone. She could gossip about anybody and anything for hours. She could have told me. She *knew*. Funny thing, I thought all the time Bonnie was my friend. But she wasn't. She was my mama-in-law's friend and put Shurli before me. Bonnie knew *everythang*. And didn't tell me. Not one goddamned word. Them niggahs was all in cahoots—they had set me up to get EarlRay off parole by marryin' him off to me. So he could run the streets without having to look over his shoulders for the Law. That was the goddamned dirty trick they put me in.

Your mother-in-law Shurli and her friend Bonnie encouraged Earl-Ray's relationship with you.

Right. He had done sumpthin', they said, I done forgot what, and they brought him by the house and begged me to let him spend a few days there until he cooled off and the police quit lookin' for him. I call myself helpin' out friends. I didn't know that was a lie concocted to get her son into my panties. They knew how lonely I was and they knew how to school him to appeal to me. They knew what my tastes were and what I would respond to favorably. I'd known them bitches for over a decade. But I'd never met EarlRay till that night they brought him by. And I can just hear them tellin' him how to act around me to seduce me, now that I look back on it. Those dog-ass niggah bitches ruined my life and my children's lives. All the time, pretending they were my hope-to-die buddies.

This is a convoluted story. I'm not sure I'm getting everything in order. What was it about EarlRay that you didn't know, that these various individuals were supposed to inform you about?

Please let me tell it in my own way.

No offense intended Dr. Flowers, but I was always the type of person prided myself on my friendships. Understand? I mean, the idea of havin' ta pay somebody like you to be my professional friend, so to speak, I thought *that* was the insanity. I guess I really believed that Golden Rule shit they taught us in grade school. About doing unto others as you would have others do unto you. That was jes' pure-dee indoctrination. Didn't have effin' beans to do with reality.

In my opinion, my husband was the one who needed the psychiatrist. When I suggested it, Shurli said she knew this brother who was also a professor at one of the top local universities. I shoulda known sumpthin' was wrong just from that, cuz in them days institutions like that only hired hanky-brained Negroes. Once I went along and waited for EarlRay in the outer office during the visit—he usually went alone—but I didn't speak to the shrink cuz I didn't think our marriage was the issue. Lo and behold.

What did you think were EarlRay's issues?

Changing his way of thinkin' so he could stay off the dope and stay out of jail. Workin' on his self-esteem. It's hard enough being a Black man in this town when you look like one. When you don't—that's truly a killer. And most people when they look at EarlRay assume he's just a funny-colored White boy, a Latino, or an S.A.

S.A.?

South American. And that was when he was by himself. But when we were paired up, the party really started.

I'm sorry, I don't follow you.

Every one of EarlRay's attempts to establish himself by gettin' a good job was sabotaged by racists.

In what way?

I had warned EarlRay that it would happen. But he wouldn't believe it.
See—EarlRay would go out and spend hours beatin' the pavement till he found a job as a fry cook. That was his only skill. He could cook his ass off on them hot griddles in some café or fast food joint. Then he start workin', provin' himself to his employer—White, Jew, or Armenian as the case might be. Then he'd be so proud of himself! And he wanted to show off how good he was doin' on the job. So he'd invite me down to the place so he could cook sumpthin' for me to enjoy, then come and sit with me at the table durin' his break. Some-times, he'd be the little boss, havin' one or two Mexicans workin' under him.
But the minute they saw us together, and realized I was his wife, he was fired within forty-eight hours—usually less than that. Some-times that very night. He'd come home with his paycheck or sever-ance cash and say he was never going back.

Maybe it was more complex a situation than you're assuming, Mrs. Jackson. Maybe it was something EarlRay was doing that got him fired.

I thought of that. Granted, EarlRay is a till-tapper and a liar. But I could tell by the way he became so troubled and depressed afterwards. And angry to the point of tears. He was tellin' me the truth.

What makes you so certain?

That's a typical event in the lives of mixed-race couples. I've known it to happen before to others. The fact that we weren't a mixed-race couple but only looked like one made it all the more ironic and hurtful. It meant he was denied his chance to prove himself a man according to what this society says a man should be—the breadwinner of the family.

And the other way I knew he was tellin' the truth was because after they fired him he would cool his heels for a couple of weeks and then go back and burglarize the joint. What he couldn't get out of the safe, the freezer, or the supply closet, he made up for in destroyin' equipment and furnishings. When he'd come in with the stuff, I'd ask him where he got it. He'd make this funny smirk and say he'd been out issuin' payback. But that still left him out of a job. And he was tryin' to walk the narrow, if not so straight.

May we backtrack a moment?

Let's—let's examine that startling point you raised about EarlRay's mother. Given the period in which you first met her, there was considerable consciousness-raising going on about relationships between women—across racial and economic lines. Were you part of that energy?

Feminism. Yeah. I was at the forefront. And that's how I came to hook up with Shurli and Bonnie. I met them at one of my after-school hangouts in the late sixties. A gathering place for women artists. You know, I was pretty stupid when it comes to homosexuality—male or female. My parents had raised me to believe it was wrong like they say in the Bible. But I dismissed that as soon as I could read on my own. Them days I was so driven by my own agenda, I frankly didn't give it much thought. I just accepted people at face value till they showed me it was unwise. So when I met Shurli and Bonnie, it was in a culturally rich environment. Folks was lettin' it all hang out, as the sayin' went. I called myself bein' a free spirit. So women with beards and women kissin' women didn't even make me blink. I just bogarted on, focused on my working-ass-poor business. Thinkin' I was gonna overthrow this and overthrow that. So it never occurred to me that maybe Shurli and Bonnie might be funny bunnies.

What?

Bisexuals. I didn't care. Remember, I was a practitioner of the Golden Rule. And when I was in their company, they always played it straight. If they were droppin' any lugs—or hints—I wasn't catchin' on. I was just enjoying being high off the energy of women speakin' their minds and behinds—as Shurli used to say. Bonnie and Shurli were fifteen or sixteen years my senior and I enjoyed my role as the baby. They would school me about the entertainment business, the ins and outs, as well as the political underground. It was an excitin' time filled with marches and demonstrations and guerrilla theatre. Sumpthin' was constantly goin' on.

Those were the ten years before meeting Shurli's son, EarlRay.

Yeah. The movement evaporated. But I still kept in touch with Bonnie and Shurli. Especially Bonnie. She was dark-skinned like me, and we had more in common when it came to ambition. There was sumpthin' about Shurli that I couldn't like, deep down, and I didn't know what it was at the time.

To use your own description of the process, you couldn't read or interpret Shurli's motives or her true nature or vibes. Your friend Bonnie further confused you by deceiving you about Shurli.

It came down to that. I kept my distance, stopping by to see Shurli once in a while. But it was Bonnie who kept drawing us together. Since they were the elders, I acquiesced. It's quite a compliment to a young person when the older folk let you run with 'em. Ummm . . . you're at least twenty years my junior, Dr. Flowers?

Uh–yes. Exactly. We could be mother and daughter under different circumstances.

So you were born about the end of the sixties, right? Missed it all.

Well–I certainly heard about it. As has everyone by now.

Yeah. Well what you heard 'tain't necessarily the way things went down on the black-hand side. I haven't seen an accurate portrayal of it yet and don't expect to see it in my lifetime, anyhow. That's why I wanted to be a filmmaker. To tell my stories the way I wanted, rather than to have some misinterpretation made of my truth. But it was economic racism that kept me from makin' the kind of money I needed to finish school. And when I was in school, I run up against racist professors in the department who weren't gonna teach me jack shit.
   You're not from out here, are you Dr. Flowers?

No. I'm not, although I'm not thoroughly ignorant about the west. I was raised in the east, did pre-grad at Arizona University and finished at Spellman, where I taught for awhile–in the Atlanta area–before taking up my practice.

I bet your parents are proud of you–got that dipolma framed, Dr. Sandra H. Flowers–bold and in gold.

Yes. They did have it framed for me as a gift.
   I assure you, I know the ins and outs of racism quite well. I grew up quite involved in my community. Then my professional pursuits brought me here.

You were lucky. I can tell. Black had become beautiful by the time you were born. Your people loved you. They weren't ashamed of you. They didn't call you ugly names until it made you sick in the stomach. Your looks were considered pretty. You have a good grade of hair. Your skin is the color of lightly browned toast with butter. And you've got that Ivy-League air to boot.

You're getting at?

Life was the opposite for me with my generation. Out here in the west, all the niggahs my age and older were at root usually ashamed of their color if they were dark, or put at a disadvantage because of it. My family was a bunch of color-struck Negroes. My classmates, largely migrants from the Deep South, were far worse. They festered with self-hate. I had a bad grade of hair and was the color of burnt toast. I was considered ugly. EarlRay's psychiatrist was of my genera- tion and blacker than me. Underneath his cosmopolitan pose was all that shame and horror of self-hate, and I spotted it right off and he knew it. We didn't have to speak a word about that, it's back-alley deep. I tried to ignore it because I truly needed his help. But he knew I knew, was wounded by it, and started takin' it out on me despite himself. Besides, EarlRay had been bright-skinned. So he assumed I was as color-struck as he was, thinkin' I only liked bright-skinned men when nuthin' could be further from the truth.

That is quite an analysis: a leap and a summary. But you had begun addressing your relationship with Shurli and Bonnie—girlfriends who became more intimate when you married Shurli's son. Since they were much older than you, and of varying complexions, you're imply- ing that, as with EarlRay's psychiatrist, the color-consciousness phe- nomenon also tainted your relationships with those women?

Bingo. Bonnie was deferential to Shurli because she was light-skinned. Shurli didn't think much of my ambition to be a filmmaker. Their so- called friendship and sisterhood had largely been jive. But they thought I'd make a good wife and housekeeper. It was EarlRay they were looking out for. They wanted a caretaker for him. I was elected and groomed. They didn't give a damn about me, my dream, or my kids. My so-called feminist sistuhs.

You're making very strong statements about your mother-in-law Shurli and your girlfriend Bonnie without grounding them in anything factual.

The facts are some horrible shit. I live with it in my head every day. That's what's brought me here to you. I need to let it out so my brain will go back to normal—if it can.

What is it that these women knew that they did not tell you? Mrs. Jackson, are you all right?

Yeah.

Do you need a moment? Go ahead. Take the time you need.

They—uh—didn't tell me—uh—that—uh—EarlRay was a child molester.

Ahh! Oh. I'm sooo sorry, Mrs. Jackson.
    How terribly difficult for you. That is quite a horrendous thing to discover about the man you love and are married to.

And get pregnant by. And have his child. And thinkin' about how happy I am, happy for the first time in my adult life. Then I come to find out sumpthin' like that. I was spinnin' around and around. I didn't know what to do. I didn't know what to do for me or my children. I didn't know who to turn to.

In desperation you went to EarlRay's psychiatrist.

EarlRay had been drug-collectin'—that's the only reason he ever went to any doctor of any kind. When Dr. Rudenik finally got some of the picture and realized EarlRay had been jerkin' his chain too, he had sense enough to get embarrassed about his behavior. He finally asked me what I wanted. I told him some pills—just a light enough dosage to take the edge off. So I could get proper sleep and go to work every day. So I could keep things together for my kids. He wrote out a prescription with ten refills and that was the last I saw of him. I wasn't about to go back to anybody who blamed me for what my husband did. I was deceived. My brain was so dead tired all the time from workin' twelve to fourteen hours a day it was easy for me to be deceived. It galled me that Dr. Rudenik couldn't appreciate that.

It's unfortunate and unfair, but the mother is usually blamed in situations like that. It is assumed that she knows but allows the ugliness to continue, out of fear and/or denial. The reasons are complex. Usually, in situations like that, the molester leaves clues or insights to his behavior. He warns his victim before he strikes, like the hissing of a snake. The molester often takes the failure of the victim—in your case, the mother—to read these warnings as tacit *permission* to commit the transgression. The perpetrator thereby justifies such untoward behavior.

Gotcha. I could see evidence of that when I looked back on it. But I couldn't see it when I was in it. Too many distractions. I was constantly under siege by this racist survival madness—tryin' to keep 'em from cuttin' off one utility or another, jugglin' the bills, dealin' with gettin' that slumlord to fix or repair this, that, or the other thing, tryin' to raise my kids right, get 'em in the right school and deal with their medical problems, fendin' off nosy racist neighbors, and on and on. Not to mention tryin' to have sumpthin' of a life for myself. Tryin' to go back to school to get my degree in cinema. Crackin' them books. Me thinkin' I could be some big shot woman filmmaker someday. And can't even look out for my own children no matter how hard I try.

Child molestation is not limited to the underclasses, Mrs. Jackson. Let me assure you. Mothers of all economic stripes have suffered this scourge.

Yeah. But women with privilege get offered help and women with money can afford to buy help. They can do *sump-thin'* about their situation. Rich and middle-class women get all the attention and what little sympathy's goin' around. I mean, what was I supposed to do? I had an eighteen-month-old baby, and two kids in puberty, was working two jobs—night and day, and squeezing in classes in between—thinkin' I was gonna be somebody.

What signs did EarlRay give you, about his behavior—in retrospect?

One of the lugs he dropped was when we went to see Miguel Piñero's play *Short Eyes*. I was always draggin' EarlRay to plays and shit. Runnin' with the hip Hollywood underground. It would blow EarlRay's mind. He was intimidated by ordinary folk like us hangin' around movie stars and industry people. It made him jumpy. So we got comps to see *Short Eyes* which is about how child molesters—men who have eyes for the short ones, or children, are ultimately dealt with by the straight convicts who detest them. EarlRay nearly had a heart attack. But I assumed that was because the play was so powerful and graphic. Not because he was identifyin' with the child-molester prisoner who gets murdered by fellow inmates.

Coincidentally—and this really gets me—about six weeks before I found out, one of the local TV stations—KCOW—did one of those investigative series on that very topic. EarlRay and me watched the series together. We actually laid up in bed in front of the TV every afternoon the entire week. He would come in and I'd be watchin' and he'd hop in right beside me. After they'd show sumpthin', he'd ask me what I'd do if thus-and-so jumped off. And I said, "I'd kill the MF." And he wouldn't say anything, and I took that to mean he agreed with my opinion. When I think back on it, he was givin' me clues all right. I just couldn't see 'em.

So when I realized what he was doin' to my kids, I called the TV station. They had kept flashing a helpline number, supposed to be. They gave me the number and I called it.

What happened?

Just like with Cane's group. I got one of those stupid-ass White women who think they own the world. No street smarts at all. When I told her straight-out what my husband had done and that I needed advice, do you know what that idiot told me?

What?

CALL THE POLICE. To call the very muthafuckin' authorities that didn't help me out in the first goddamned place. As if the police would do anything to help me. I was also asking for help for EarlRay. To my way of thinkin', he needed a doctor, not to be locked up again. At that point, for all I knew, it might have been all that time spent in the slammer that warped his mind. I knew he had been jail-raped, cuz he told me about that. But I thought the love of a good woman would help him get past it. Why would I want the police to come in here and arrest EarlRay and ruin any chance to work out the situation for the best?

She didn't know who she was talkin' to. She couldn't even begin to appreciate the relationship between Black folk and the police who have traditionally enforced the laws that have held us down. Couldn't no police help us no way possible. Plus, she didn't know my personal experience with callin' the police. Whenever I have done that, I have been laughed at—by them. No matter how serious the situation was with me. You have no idea what it feels like when you go to the authorities and beg them for help and they laugh in your face and tell you *you deserve* the misery you got.

I tried to get that across to her. She said she wouldn't help me if I didn't go to the police *first*. So I hung up in the bitch's face. Not that that gave me any satisfaction. I was still spinnin' round and round.

Then EarlRay ran off.

You had confronted him with the situation?

Oh yeah. Right away. I didn't realize it then, but I was in shock. I tried to talk through it. But I was in a daze that lasted nearly two weeks. I started wakin' up in the middle of the night and starin' at EarlRay for minutes at a time, not sayin' nuthin'. I started thinkin' about stabbin' EarlRay to death. He must've heard my thoughts. I was tryin' to stay nice to him. Keep him from runnin' till I could figure it all out. What would happen to my kids? That they had been molested was horrible enough. Now they were about to be orphaned and they Mama in jail for murdering her child-molester husband. All that kept goin' through my mind. How they would most likely end up in the same institutions that had warped EarlRay. How they would be victimized and brutalized cuz they wouldn't have any of the protection I provided, even if it was meager protection. It had been better than nuthin'. I was thinkin' like that. Round and around. Plus realizin' that the love I had for that booger was still in my heart. Child molestation's the worst betrayal of trust there is. I had to somehow get that betrayed love out of my system. Not to mention, if I didn't go to jail, I still had had his baby. And I was gonna have to live with that fact all the rest of my days. Who was gonna raise the baby? And one day, I was gonna have to tell that child that his father was a child molester. And what kind of impact was that gonna have on that innocent little boy? That little boy I loved heart and soul. And how would I explain to my older kids, who were equally my heart and soul, why mother didn't just cut the muthafucka's throat from the get-go and keep movin'?

Did you share this information with Shurli and Bonnie?

With Bonnie. All the while not knowin' my so-called feminist buddies were culpable. Especially Shurli.

What do you mean—culpable?

Shurli was a child molester herself. That evil bitch had molested all of her children. The boys *and* the girls.

My God!

Bonnie told me this—way after the fact. EarlRay and one of his sisters, and one of Shurli's old boyfriends confirmed it. Bonnie had known all along, from way back, before I had ever met the bitches. She apologized and said she was in denial or whatever. But fact is, she knew and did not tell me. If she had've I'd've *nevah* let that man through my door, or Shurli for that matter. Then she told me EarlRay was constantly at her place beggin' her to have sex with him. She said she just couldn't and told him not to come there. She said that's why she talked to me so much on the phone but discouraged us dropping over. So here I am drownin' and she dumps more salt water on me.

This Bonnie person—her bizarre behavior was certainly sadistic and indicates she had little sympathy for your plight. The worst possible time to tell a woman that her husband has been cheating on her is when she's just found out he's molested her children. It's obvious that this Bonnie was never your friend by any stretch of the word.

What about Shurli?

I never confronted Shurli about her evil self—about what she did to her own children or what she had done to mine by proxy. I never spoke to her after that, in fact, now that I recall. I was too hurt and too distraught. She was the last person I wanted to see next to EarlRay. Bonnie acted as the go between. Bonnie told her I knew. Bonnie told me she knew I knew. I think Shurli stayed away cuz she suspected I might kill EarlRay and kill her too.

How did you find out? Who told you EarlRay was molesting your children? Mrs. Jackson, are you hearing me? Who told you about EarlRay?

That's the strangest part of it all, Dr. Flowers.

One of the children told you?

No. However, I did find a letter to God written by my son. I confronted EarlRay with it. But that was not the way I found out. That letter simply confirmed what I had just discovered the evening before.

What's wrong Mrs. Jackson? Why are you hesitating?

Trust is as much a part of the relationship between doctor and patient as it is between husband and wife—or friends. I don't want to lie to you. But I don't want the truth to cast doubt or suspicion on what I've told you. So help me—everything I've told you is God's honest truth, even if colored by my perception. It's important to me that you believe me. So I'm stuck now—in a dangerous place.

You're afraid I won't believe you.

Yeah.

Try me. Trust me. Trust the fact that I've listened to you, uncritically, for the entire time you've sat here before me. I've done my utmost to offer you the professionalism you say you were denied by others. I'm not a liar either—if capable of lying, the same as anyone. More importantly, if we continue to trust one another, perhaps you'll be able to resume your day-to-day life with much more hope and enthusiasm.

Thank you, Dr. Flowers. I appreciate that.

Good. I'm human too, but very broadminded. Shall we try it again? Who told you that EarlRay was molesting your children?

The walls told me.

What?

The walls told me, Dr. Flowers.

I—I'm sorry. Please tell me what occurred, in detail.

One of the big bosses had some big celebration across town and they closed the office early without notice and sent the help home. Earl-Ray had kept the car that day and was supposed to pick me up from work. He wasn't home to get my phone call, and nobody answered at his brother's pad or Shurli's. It was just a twenty-minute hop from our

113

place, so I took the bus and walked the half block to the apartment. The kids were still in school. With EarlRay out in the streets job huntin', I figured it would be a rare opportunity for me to put in some quality study time. I was startin' to fall behind in my reading assignments. When I got to the door, I got a jolt when I turned the key in the lock. I figured it was just static electricity. Later when I looked at the key, it was melted where metal touched metal. Then I turned the knob and went inside. See, our apartment was on the top floor, and we had to climb a full flight of stairs. I looked around for loose wires, but I couldn't see any. As I mounted the stairs, I heard these voices talking to me in sync.

More than one?

Yes.

What did these voices say?

They said, "He's bothering the children."

That's all?

Yes. That one sentence. Nothing else.

What did you say?

Nothing. I stood there stunned. It made me sick to my soul. Then I ran up the rest of the stairs and started searching the place to see if there wasn't someone in there playing tricks on me. But there was no one there but me. That meant one of two things—either the walls had actually talked or I was having a nervous breakdown. And I didn't know how to deal with either conclusion. I'm not big on spookism. And I was less enthusiastic about madness.

What did you do?

I tried to reason my way through it. But I didn't have time. The kids came in. That meant seeing to it that they changed clothes and got into their homework. And then EarlRay came in after them. That meant doing all my usual chores before having time to study. And I had to start dinner. So I put on a front like nothing had happened. EarlRay noticed the front door lock had a burn notched into it and was blackened by smoke. The smell of singed metal still lingered on the air. I explained to him about the key. He looked at it and whistled, saying I was lucky I wasn't electrocuted. But he couldn't figure out why it had happened either.

You didn't tell him about the voices?

No. I didn't. I've never told anyone about those voices. You're the first. When I found the letter the next day, I didn't need to tell him about hearing any voices. I had sumpthin' concrete to confront him with. Besides, trying to explain why I was hearing voices would've taken away from what I felt was the more serious issue. Voices or no voices, I had a child molester on my hands.

Yes. Your decision was the correct one.

So what now, Dr. Flowers? Do you think I'm a mental case?

No. I don't. I think there's a very logical explanation for the phenomenon you experienced. As you said, I'm not big on spookism either. And I'm not yet ready to equate the power of prayer with what's popularly known as the supernatural. Yet—if I accept you at your word— you heard the walls speak.

As clear as you're speaking right now. No distortion.

Were the voices male or female?

I couldn't tell. They didn't have any gender, or any accent for that matter.

115

And you're certain they came from the walls? And not inside your head?

I was climbing the stairs, and they came from above my head, out of the walls—the exterior wall of the kid's room. I was looking at that wall. Then the voices came.

The same room in which you found your son's note to God?

Yeah. I was runnin' the vacuum cleaner the next evening. I had removed the rug brush and was using the nozzle to reach hard places when it became clogged by a sheet of paper. I pulled it out and noticed my son's handwriting. It looked like a fledgling love letter so I started reading it. He was pleading to God to make EarlRay leave him and his sister alone. That letter left me no choice. I sat EarlRay down and showed it to him.

How did he react?

I don't remember. I don't remember his face or what he said. None of that. It's all a blank now. I don't remember what I said to him or the kids—except that I tried to get everybody to talk about it. But nobody was talkin' except me, and I'm not sure how much sense I was makin'. I knew we had to have outside help. And I started tryin' to figure out how we were going to get it—how we were going to get through the nightmare, now that everything was out in the open. How was I going to go to work every day knowin' this molester was in the house? And even though he was exposed, he still might do more harm to my kids if left there alone with them. How could I—as the one supportin' us— keep my job without crackin' up?

Did you tell your family?

Them color-struck Negroes? Hell no. The last thing I needed was to have them crowing and cawin' and tellin' me that's what I get for mar- ryin' an ex-convict.

116

Dr. Flowers—how do you explain those voices? Was it me? Or was it sumpthin' else?

Without a doubt, it was you, Mrs. Jackson.

How so?

All humans possess the skill of deductive reasoning to one degree or another. In this instance, the hints—or lugs as you call them—dropped by EarlRay had registered on your subconscious mind. You had read and understood them on a subliminal level. You deduced the truth. However, the horror of the realization and your repulsion were so extreme your conscious mind couldn't accept the knowledge and remain functional. You could not afford to shut down mentally or emotionally. Too much was at stake, particularly the welfare of your children. Therefore, the information was blocked, trapped between your subconscious mind and your conscious, waking mind. That blockage allowed you to remain rational during your waking state, while the truth raged in your subconscious.

My brain was constipated?

It was a form of self-defense, similar to the process that takes place in the development of multiple personalities. To your credit, you were actually too sane to succumb or break down completely. The incident with the key served as a catalyst, so to speak—the physical shock became a conduit for the mental shock. The two together produced the two voices you heard. They came from above you, because your brain, as you call it—in whatever state of confusion you were in—was focused on the wall of your children's room where the acts of molestation took place, as were your eyes as you climbed the stairs. Hence, the walls spoke.

And what would you call that in psychological terms?

A mild temporary psychosis—as a working diagnosis. Perhaps a rare form of what's known as episodic reactive schizophrenia. Either would

117

account for the hallucination of talking walls. You weren't using drugs were you?

No. That was sumpthin' EarlRay liked about me. He wanted our baby to be born without any abnormalities, he claimed. My system was "clean," he always said—meanin' drug-free. And durin' the time we were workin' on conceivin' he promised me he was keepin' his system clean of everything—except cigarettes. He had a serious smokin' habit —one to two packs a day. After the baby was born, he went back to smokin' marijuana and whatever else he and his crimies could get into. I was constantly exposed to marijuana smoke, especially at night, on weekends, when EarlRay had company. He ran with a pretty rowdy crowd. I'd play hostess, servin' drinks and snacks, but I didn't smoke with 'em. EarlRay would tease me afterwards, tellin' me I had gotten a contact high—takin' in the smoke just by bein' in the same room.

Where were your kids when these parties were going on?

Sleep in their room way down the hall. With the baby, after he was born. I kept the door to their room shut. Plus, we'd have the livin' room door shut, the windows open, the fans goin', and incense burnin'. I didn't want the kids exposed to it. EarlRay respected my wishes in that regard. Do you think my being exposed to marijuana could have contributed to the split in my psyche?

I honestly don't know. There simply isn't any reliable research available on that sensitive issue—just yet. And I'm not certain of that—it is distinctly outside my field of study. But—given what's known in the popular culture—it's highly likely that there was some residual influence, since, according to the literature, marijuana stays in one's system in excess of six months.

For real, Dr. Flowers?

For real, Mrs. Jackson. Are you comfortable with my assessment of your behavior so far?

So the situation with EarlRay drove me temporarily insane, is that it?

I can't say so with absolute certainty. But it's a good place to start, in terms that may have therapeutic value to you.

Hah! I've waited a long time to talk this thing out, Dr. Flowers. I don't know whether that's good news or bad.

How are you feeling now—emotionally?

I don't know. Relieved ain't quite the word for it. Talkin' about all this has brought it to the surface. I feel sore. Like when you get a splinter deep under the skin. If you don't get it out, it seems to heal. Know what I mean? The pain goes away as if the splinter's gone. But it's there all along. And a week or two later, you look at the site and notice it's all white with infection caused by the splinter. You can see the splinter fairly floatin' in pus. The interestin' thing is that the pus makes it easier to remove the splinter—take a needle and you can lift it out real easy. Or you can squeeze it with your fingers and express the splinter and the pus. Then all you need to do is wash the wound clean and apply disinfectant or a bandage. After you do that, the site is sore for a little while—until the new healing takes place. That's what my brain feels like now. A bit sore from bein' squeezed.

That's an apt analogy. I'll take that as a compliment. If the splinter remained in your system, so to speak, it could become poisonous and lead to complications. The infection, those white cells that have gathered, is your body's defenses, the act of saving yourself. I think it's an amazing feat that you've literally starved yourself in order to raise the money to help yourself. I've simply been a means of your *expression*, to double the meaning of the word.

What EarlRay was doin' to my kids was like a splinter in my brain.

Yes. That's a remarkably balanced and restrained way to state it. Let's stay with that analogy of yours. That splinter was more on the order

119

of a spear. Therefore, it is a testament to your strength of character that you survived it at all. Many don't do as well.

You're talking about the murder-suicides.

Or the suicides. Or simply the murderers—the women who end up in prison for killing their spouses. That kind of violence creates a sensation in the media and occasionally elevates a woman to celebrity status. She becomes a heroine. Ironically, seldom is such a woman from the African-American underclass. I agree with you that our society is racist. However, the average woman—Brown, Black, Yellow, or White —who commits such an act is banished from society—incarcerated without sympathy from the outside world which, I'm sad to say, remains male-dominated. She's killed her man—even if justified—and must be punished without regard to mitigating factors, particularly when those factors are psychological in nature.

You're talking about another ugly double standard—one people don't like to talk about. All those tabloid people who fantasize about sex acts with children and who get off on hearin' and talkin' about it.

I'm afraid that's a larger part of our culture than the average American likes to admit. Despite our social climate of increasing confessional openness, it is still largely a taboo subject. Some victims live with it in silence. They turn inward or escape by denying that the molestation took place.

That explains why my brain has been so tired all this time. Its been battlin' the silence. Even though I've fought it and fought it all these years—tryin' not to let the depression stop me from functioning. Most of the time, things seem normal. Then it comes on like a tsunami, and I get seriously down in the dumps. Is there a term for that?

Its called psycholepsy.
    You're quiet again, Mrs. Jackson. Judging by the clock, our time together is at an end. Would you like to continue our sessions?

120

Yes. I'd love to, Dr. Flowers. But I don't know if I should.

We could work something out, regarding my fee—if you like?

No. No, I believe in folks bein' paid for the work that they do. It's just that—

Just that—what?

Our age difference—you being of one generation, me being so much older. I've found that women your age are more fully developed as feminists than my generation. You've naturally become more of what we aspired to be—because attitudes did change some, if not enough. You're the embodiment, in a way, of our dream. You're confident and successful without all the messy stuff.

I don't follow you. What does age have to do with our doctor-patient relationship?

Trust is trust, regardless of the demographics.

It's just that I wouldn't want you comin' up with some kind of screwball analysis of me—like bra-burning-itis or sixties neurosis or some such. When I talk about the past, you know? I can't help when I was born.

Well, that's something you needn't worry about, Mrs. Jackson. I'm not EarlRay's rudenik shrink—as you so aptly called him. I pride myself on keeping my personal biases in check. I want to do as much as I can to be of help.

Just the words I want to hear. I've saved up enough for maybe another few sessions. If you can hang with me?

That's quite an expression, Mrs. Jackson. More on the order of a double entendre with a Freudian twist.

Freudian twist? That's a new one.

We'll talk more about that at the top of our next session. I'll ink you in right now. Next week at the same time. Here's your appointment card as a reminder, Mrs. Jackson.

Thank you, Dr. Flowers.

No sweat—as they say in the ghetto. Yes—I can and will hang with you. For as long as the rope holds and until the posse arrives. Shall we shake hands on that?

Shake.

My Son,
My Son

IF THE NIGHT wasn't dead, it was certainly in the throes.

Carlos Brown sat listless and blue behind the wheel of his franchised bright green and yellow taxicab, a retooled late-model sedan. It was parked at the shopping mall taxi stand, beacon off for service. His day's tired crashed on him. Sick with apprehension, he anticipated his hardened supervisor's habitual nasty cracks about his continued failure to exceed his daily rental minimum, thereby having spent yet another day's work without making a dollar to feed his family. Carlos's failing was that of the decent man caught in corrupt circumstances. He didn't have the stomach or the predatory nerve to hustle fares whether they were well heeled or otherwise.

It wasn't his fault the high-desert boomtown had gone bust. It wasn't his fault that the failure of elected officials to score lucrative government contracts had depressed the town's economy. And it was not his fault that, in a town thriving on used vehicles, there were more undereducated guys down on their luck trying to make their living as cabbies than there were passengers needing the costly service.

The sack lunch he had wolfed between late fares had disagreed with his digestive tract. Each soft belch tasted like rancid baloney, moldy American cheese, and bitter apple. Despite the battery's threats to die and leave him stranded, he shunned monitoring the dispatcher's calls, which were seldom his anyway and, between a flurry of concerns, absorbed the pulsations of Christmas songs played disco-style over a local radio station.

Sleepily, he lowered his yellow driver's cap over his eyes, slid down in the seat and went into a nod. The morning's conversation with Ramona bubbled up in his heart. They had argued in harsh whispers and hisses but sensed the children listening quietly beyond closed doors. Would there ever be a Christmas that wasn't celebrated at midnight, after father came home from some spirit-sucking drudge? Would there ever be a Christmas when the tree was not scrawny and old, the gifts cheap and unwanted, the feast cheerless and forced?

Tapppity-taptaptapppity-tap!

His eyes snapped in the direction of the sharp sounds. There was no one at the passenger's window. Carlos pulled himself upright and looked again.

Tapppity-taptaptapppity-tap!

It was at his left ear.

Angrily, he twisted around to give the knocking idiot a whole new vocabulary. But an unseemly specter disarmed and disturbed him.

The driver's pane was filled with the striking head of an old charcoal-skinned crone with a bushy beard of off-white chin whiskers. She was rapping the window with the silver head of her cane held in one of her gnarled paws with six-inch talons painted fire engine red. Her hair was a witch's broom of black, silver and off-white wires snaking in every direction. Her large recessed eyes peered out at him from under extravagant lashes, skin folds and cavernous shadows. She wore too much face powder, which gave her leathery complexion a ghostly reddish cast. Her bridgeless nose sprang forward like a smooth, porous promontory. Her mustachioed lips were bizarrely well shaped and painted into a red permanent smooch. Stretched apart in a smile, they revealed half-rotted teeth with two red-stained incisors capped in gold. Carlos had the uneasy impression that she had once been a larger, heavy-set woman who had somehow shrunk.

Before he could respond, she waddled curbside as if to hail a rival. Carlos collected himself, stepped out, and went after her.

"Need a taxi, ma'am?"

"Young man! You look like an honest young man." In contrast to her appearance, her voice sounded young and oddly sensual. She fairly danced with agitation, lugged an old carpetbag, scrawny bowed legs in ill-fitting nylons knotted at knobby knees under her tattered, ancient, full-length fur coat.

"I'm in a hurry! A hurry, I say."

"Yes, ma'am. What can I do—something to help?"

"I've got to get to the airport! Immediately."

"Which airport, ma'am."

"International. My son's coming home."

Carlos brightened. Ordinarily, the metered one-way drive in heavy traffic would take a maximum of two tension-choked hours. Round trip, the fare would be enormous. Such a trip this time of evening would be laid back—provided she could pay.

"That's a mighty expensive trip, ma'am. Are you sure?"

"Sure I'm sure."

"Did you want to go one way?"

"Round trip! Hurry, we'll be late!"

She bustled toward the back door. He leapt ahead of her and opened it. She crawled in, and he closed it snugly behind her.

"Please fasten your seat belt, ma'am!" Carlos reminded her as he climbed behind the wheel, his better sense tugging at his wallet. Reluctantly he hit the beacon and radioed in the fare, watching her in the rearview mirror. She wrestled with the seat belt, clamped the metal buckle head with the meat of her palms and bent fingers, careful of those curved talons. Suppose he drove all the way to the airport only to discover she was every pound the nursing-home lunatic she looked? He would be out his night's pay with no way to recuperate the loss in regular fares. He decided to try the tactic used when a fare is undesirable.

"I'm sorry ma'am, you'll have to pay in advance."

"In advance?"

"Yes, ma'am."

He twisted around and watched her plumb the depths of the old carpetbag. She came up with a fistful of bills. Without managing to shred his palms with her nails, she showered the bills over his hands, the front seat, and clipboard log. Quickly, Carlos collected them, counted them, and whistled.

"Ma'am—it won't cost you anywhere's near this much!"

"Keep the change, young man. And hurry!"

"Yes, sir—uh, ma'am!"

Carlos felt the rush head to foot. Eagerly, he fired the engine, set the radio dial on the easy-listening station and took the shortest street route to the freeway, due south.

On the road, a spectacular moonrise illuminated the rocky eastern terrain. The town's landscape of lights receded, and stars blanketed what could be seen of the western horizon above canyon walls as the sleek taxicab clipped along soothingly to the seasonal music just above the posted speed limit.

Settled into the drive, Carlos hummed along between periodic glances in the rearview to see whether or not his eerily silent, troll-like fare had vanished in a puff of weirdness. Partly in amusement, partly out of curiosity, the usually taciturn Carlos broached communication.

"So, your son's coming home for Christmas. That must make you very happy."

"Yes. My son is coming home." She blinked at the passing panorama.

"Your son, he works overseas—huh?"

"My son teaches English at a secondary school in Hong Kong. My son was recently in Naples for an arts and culture convention. My son's diplomatic post in Brussels has been very exciting. My son frequently travels Central and South America collecting antiquities. My son's appointment to represent our community at the Pan African Congress was very exciting."

"Wow! Some guy! Where'd he go to school?"

"My son was a 4-letter man, Jefferson High varsity. My son graduated magna cum laude from State University. My son did his post-graduate studies at Stanford. My son attended adult school religiously, working nights until he received his certificate of completion. Med-

126

ical school was a particular challenge, but my son weathered it, as I knew he would. Dropping out of school at such a tender age was very difficult, but my son grew up fast. When my son's tour of duty ended, he was the first to reenlist."

"Uh-huh!" Carlos wasn't sure he had heard correctly, but then he could only half-listen, his main focus on the road. "So is he married? Any grandchildren?"

"My son and his lovely wife recently celebrated their thirtieth anniversary, their children are grown and they have children."

"That makes you a great grandmother—huh?"

"My son married his childhood sweetheart, they went to high school together; she couldn't give birth, so they've adopted two children and it's worked out well. My son has lived a bachelor's life, but seems happy enough. I warned my son not to let divorce make him bitter, his ex-wife getting full custody of their son and daughter was not the end of the world. My son and his significant other seem content to live on the fringe of society."

"Excuse me?"

"My son's in construction and built a lovely home for himself. My son owns a hillside vacation townhouse, one of those split-level affairs, a gift to his wife. I've tried to talk my son into giving up that apartment downtown and renting in a better part of the city. I don't know why my son and his wife insist on renting in the ghetto, as if it's some test of courage. When my son wanted to move to the suburbs, it took months to find a decent real estate agent to handle the property. I couldn't imagine my son living on a houseboat, but the marina is quite beautiful, if exclusive.

"My son says they have three lovely German shepherds, show dogs with long coats and pedigrees. Five cats are simply too many, given the size of my son's apartment, and cats have such disgusting habits. It's just like my son's children to try and teach parrots foul language. I told my son that I would expect maintaining a koi pond would be a great deal of work. My son's terrarium is the largest I've ever seen, but lizards and newts as pets seem in questionable taste."

Carlos had apparently pricked open the psychic boil of her madness. Short of silence, he lapsed into automatic grunts and uh-huhs, his own doubts superceding her ramblings. He could cut this short by driving in a few circles then returning to the mall. But what if she actually had a son to meet? What if she noticed his ruse, got angry, and filed a complaint with the company? Why give that itchy asshole of a sadistic super a chance to fire him? They were nearly thirty minutes into their descent toward the coastal basin. So what if he burned a little high-performance juice?

"My son's career has really taken off, although I've warned him that rock stars and high-fashion models seldom last beyond five years. When my son tried to get into the production end, I warned him that poor distribution would cripple him. My son was stubborn and wouldn't listen when I warned him about hanging out with the wrong kind of people. . ."

At odd moments, something she said awakened a recollection. He had heard that particular tone before, on the lips of an aunt, one of the grandmothers, a sister, perhaps his mother. And sometimes he heard Ramona's loving scolding of either himself or the children. *I warned you. . .*

"I hated to see my son become so cynical after his partners forced him into a vice presidency. Filing bankruptcy nearly broke my son's spirit after he had worked terribly hard at building a successful business. Running for office required more favors and financing than my son anticipated. Working as an unarmed security guard has its drawbacks, but with my son's record, there wasn't much else he qualified for. Rare is the man who's good with young children, but my son claims to be daunted by having so many female colleagues. Starting over during a recession at my son's age was quite a challenge, but the re-educational program served him well. . ."

On and on she went, like some bizarre wind-up toy, as they zipped along, taking one freeway as it intersected with another. Perhaps she had several sons, he thought. Which was quite possible for a woman of her years, which he guessed were approaching eighty. Perhaps the facts of their lives had become jumbled in her mind. He had heard of Alzheimer's but wasn't sure if her behavior was symptomatic of the disease. The music softly scored her monologue as Carlos fell silent, driving to the rhythms, eyes and thoughts on the route ahead.

Entering the valley, the air-conditioning unit was infiltrated with the smells of the road and the season, skunk kill and pollution cut by aromas from restaurants open to accommodate hungry last-minute shoppers, logs burning in fireplaces, the piney twang from Christmas-tree lots, the sweetness of goodies baked by working mothers.

The residential sectors glowed with decorative Christmas lights of every color and configuration.

Carlos relived the excitement of those hours before everyone woke for breakfast and exchanged gifts. He remembered the playful smiles of men who had died in the years since. The uncles, the grand-fathers, all the sons of the mothers he had never known who were part of his history.

Sparse late-night traffic increased in density the closer they came to the airport. Planes glistened and flittered on the southwestern horizon, ships that, indeed, seemed more like stars as they descended toward unseen landing strips.

"You're quite a driver! We're almost there! We've made excellent time, young man."

The airport exit was suddenly less than a half mile ahead. Safely, he guided the taxi to the right and joined the stream of limousines, cabs, buses and automobiles.

"My son's going to be so pleased that I was able to meet his flight on time. I've looked forward to seeing him for so long!"

Following the signs, he took the arrival level, weaving in and out of domestic traffic toward the international terminal. No sooner had he pulled to a stop than his wily passenger pushed the door open, hopped out, and waddled into the terminal.

Snatching his keys from the ignition, Carlos leapt out after her, but she had disappeared in the crowds.

Stymied, he went back to the cab and sat. Should he wait for her? There were plenty of cabs on hand. She could take any of them for the return trip. Hadn't she paid him enough for four round trips? How much money did she have in that old carpetbag?

Had she bribed him, so to speak, with her last fistful of dollars in some warped display of a wealth she didn't have? Besides, suppose she did have a flesh-and-bone son waiting for her? Carlos envisioned her hugging him, crying out, "My son! My son!" and nearly wounding him with those twisted talons. What could her son possibly look like with a mother who looked like that?

Carlos decided to set the meter of his patience. But how many minutes, considering those now lapsed, would be time enough for her to meet her son, provided he had already gone through immigration without problems? Why was he having this debate with himself? Most of the cabbies he knew would have roared off the minute the old woman had stepped over the curb. Why hadn't he? Since he had made such good time, he could afford an hour's wait or more, if necessary, and still make it home to Ramona and the kids by midnight.

He climbed behind the wheel, felt around the floor under the dashboard, and found the thermos of strong black coffee Ramona always insisted on packing. He loosened the stopper enough for the hot brew to flow as he filled the cup. The night was temperate, not cold enough for the heater, yet the heat from the cup felt good against his palms.

He watched the general commotion as he sipped, studied the faces of passersby, listened to snatches of accented talk. He read the expressions in eyes and hands—the anxiousness, excitement, satisfaction, and relief at touching ground—a mix of emotions as they rushed to and fro, wrestling with luggage, tugging children, hugging welcomers, waving hello or goodbye, jaywalking the street, hailing cabs.

No sooner had he drained his cup and recapped the thermos than the door opened and shut. His passenger crawled into the seat alone and sat silent, rolling her eyes, hands plucking nervously at each other, like the beaks of giant chickens.

"Ma'am are you okay?"

She looked out the window and gave no answer.

"Couldn't you find your son? Maybe his flight was delayed. That's a common thing that happens. All the time. We can wait around if you want. I've got plenty of time."

"I couldn't find him," she mumbled sadly.

"Maybe you went to the wrong gate. Look, why don't you tell me his name and which airline he's traveling on and I'll go see what's going on."

She shuddered and sighed, her chest making one tremulous heave and then collapsing.

"Ma'am, are you okay?"

She looked at him. Tears flowed along her cheeks and settled into dark wrinkled creases. She went into the carpetbag for a lacy kerchief and dabbed gently at her face.

"He promised," she said softly, staring off into space.

"Let me double check that for you, ma'am. I don't mind, really."

"Thank you, young man," she said finally. "But I think we'd better get back."

"Ma'am, are you sure?"

She shuddered again, dabbed at each reddened eye and nodded.

The trip back was in gravelike silence. Carlos stole glances at his passenger who moped, exuding an atmospheric pain so palpable it made his flesh crawl. Even her rambling nonsensical conversation had been better.

"So, ma'am. You should maybe call the airlines when you get home to find out what happened to your son. I'll be glad to drive you straight home since the mall's closed by now."

She seemed to brighten, nodded and gave him the cross streets.

"It's hard to spend the holidays alone. Maybe there's someone you can visit, or who could come visit you."

She seemed to be searching the sky for the moon, which was now directly overhead.

"Your son—was he your only child?"

"My son was delivered by a midwife on a night like this. My husband rushed me to the hospital after my water broke, and I was barely conscious when my son started to arrive, just as big and bouncy as you please. My son weighed nine pounds, the biggest record of any birth in our family. My son was such an adorable child that I was shocked that anyone could abandon such a little darling. My son was born in the back seat of our old Chevrolet, after I had gone into labor at the picnic. My son weighed seven pounds and eight ounces. My son was two when we took him home from the orphanage. My son was the most beautiful manchild you ever saw. . ."

She was her former self, rambling nonstop as they climbed the high-desert route back to town. The return trip was considerably faster. He would have time to run in and out of the supermarket to pick up a few extras as a surprise for Ramona. With luck, the children would be awake when he got home. He could barely wait.

The old woman's home was a modern residence located in the wealthy part of town. It was dark and seemed deserted. But when he drove up, a porch light flicked on. A brown-skinned woman–either a daughter or housekeeper–appeared at the door and held it open. He left the motor running, jumped out, ran around to the passenger's side and opened the door.

"Merry Christmas, ma'am."

"Thank you, young man!" She had pulled out another fistful of bills and waved it at him.

"Oh, no, ma'am! You've already paid your fare, more than enough."

"No son of mine," she croaked, "is going to go broke if I can help it!" She threw the bills onto the back seat, scurried past him, up the steps, and disappeared inside.

"Hey, are you her daughter?" Carlos called out.

The woman stared at him blankly for a moment, stepped inside without a word and slammed the door.

Perplexed, but in high spirits, Carlos hastily collected the bills from the back seat and stuffed them into a pocket. He stepped back behind the wheel, lowered the front windows, and sped off on his errands, taking the shortest route possible, breathing in the night and all its smells–the burning wood, the cookies baked fresh at midnight. He felt a childlike glee at the patches of glittering colored lights and decorations on all the homes as he cruised past–the poor and the grand alike, and those in between.

Christmas had never shone brighter.

Darkness

Joleatha held her mug up for another spot of coffee. She was still in her spandex and mini-skirt, bangles dangling sexily at her ears. Beverly, nude under her cherry terrycloth robe, poured the brew neatly, plopped the pot on the place mat between them, and joined her girlfriend at the table. The kitchen was located on the western side of the ghetto building, and the midday sunlight lit it dimly. Joleatha knew that she was always welcomed but sensed a tension about the room. Beverly was cloaked in a nameless aura that somehow put the two dark-skinned women at an unfamiliar distance.

The tape deck in the living room was on and the soulful strains of rhythm and blues underscored their conversation.

Somebody was a lovin' my ol' lady while I was out makin' love...

"Girl, that was a humdinger of a party last night. The house rocked."

"You didn't have to sleep in your car, Jojo. You could've come back up here."

"Honey, I woulda if I coulda."

They laughed.

"I ain't been that tore-down in many a moon. I needed some fun for a change. And I wouldn't've been so sleepy if I hadn't've stuffed my face. But I couldn't help it, Bev. Girl, can you burnnn, let me tell yah. So my intentions were to drive home—it ain't all that far. Next thing I know, I'm pushin' myself up off the tuck 'n' roll and the sun's shinin'. Good thing it's Sunday."

"I'm glad somebody enjoyed it. I was up cookin' two goddamned days. Kenny's in there still sleep. So's the kids. I jes got out the shower."

"How's you and Kenny? He seemed real uptight for a while there."

"Usual pressures. You know. But it'll be all right."

"That was some killer weed. Who*evah* brought that shit."

"One of Kenny's partners, I think. Somebody. I got a stick here, if you want."

"Bettah not. It's gonna take all night to get the kinks out my mind as it is—so I can put on my civilized face for them ugly folks on Monday."

"I heard that."

I found love on a two-way street and lost it on a lonely highway...

Beverly's mind was elsewhere in the silence that fell between them. Joleatha felt the pressure to fill it with talk.

"Bev—you make the best coffee. I can hardly drink my own."

"Jojo—Kenny was upset cuz I got raped last night."

"Ah—what?"

"I got raped."

Joleatha reached out for Beverly's hand, grasped it, and groped for something to say. Their eyes met, then Beverly looked away.

"You know how dark it gets in here sometimes?"

"Yeah. Can't see your hand in front of your face."

"Umhummm. 'Specially in our bedroom. Even with the door open. There ain't no window. You know how this cheap building is. We had all the lights off except in the bathroom on the other side of the house where the kids sleep. They got nightlights in their room. And for the party we had put red and blue bulbs in all the other sockets. Like I said, I ain't had no sleep. Once the party got underway, and everybody dancin' and eatin', I figured I'd sneak off in there and get a couple hours shut-eye. I slipped out my dress and underwear, felt around in the dark an' hung 'em on the bedpost so they'd be fresh when I got up. Then I fell asleep.

"Next thing I know, I'm jarred awake. The whole bed's shakin', and

134

I'm shakin' with it. Some man's on top of me, between my legs gruntin' and moanin'. He got quite a hang on him. I figure he don't know I'm awake, thinks I'm still passed out. I don't know what he'll do if he finds out I'm woke. So I play possum. Once he got his nut, he laid on top of me for a minute then rolled off, pulled up his pants. I stayed real still till I hear him leave the room. Then I got up, put my clothes back on, went and found Kenny, and told him."

You are everything and everything is you, oh . . .

"No wonder he was uptight. Did he catch the guy?"

"I don't know who it was—to tell him. We had a lot of people comin' through. The door was wide open. Could've been anybody—friend or stranger. I should've kept it to myself, but I wanted Kenny to know . . . just in case something else funny jumped off."

"Damn, Bev. Damn it to hell!" Joleatha slammed her fists on the table.

"When I got up this morning, I took a look around." Beverly filled another mug, sipped the steaming brew. "Wasn't nothing stolen. The kids were fine. Kenny had fell out drunk and was sleepin' in the rocker by the door, like a guard dog."

"Bev—is there anything I can do? Are you okay?"

"I was mighty upset with it at first."

"Girl—that's really horrible!" Joleatha jumped up and did a war dance on the linoleum in high-heeled boots. "Not even safe in your own goddamned bed!"

"Hold on, hold on, now." Beverly laughed warmly at her friend.

"Coulda been some *diseased* muthafucka," she plopped into the chair.

"I thought of that, Jojo. Kenny's gonna run me over to County for some tests later today. Just in case. Better safe than sorry."

"Wish there was some way to find out who it was." Jojo's eyes bounced.

"Too late now. The dirty muthafucka got away with it."

"Did he smell of any kind of shavin' lotion—anything?"

"Alcohol, cigarettes, and sweat. And everybody here was drinkin', smokin', and dancin'."

"Maybe we should ask around?"

135

Beverly shrugged. Her eyes glinted strangely, then rolled back. She looked toward the ceiling a moment before lowering her lovely chin.

When a man loves a woman, he'll sleep out in the rain . . .

"Alls a muthafucka would do is lie. Besides, we don't have the time to waste. Kenny's got to get up early tomorrow." She sighed. "So do I."

"Is there anything I can do? Want me to stay with the kids?"

"Thanks, no. No need in you getting all upset behind it."

Joleatha sensed the indefinable.

"What's happenin' with you now?"

"Right now, I'm *fine* with it." Beverly spoke in perfect coolness.

"You sure?"

"All that man took was some pussy. Coulda been a hundred times worse."

There was a lull in the music. All that could be heard was their soft intakes of breath over the faint sounds of passing traffic from the streets below.

Dunny

ONE MORNING DUNNY flew out the window and came down to earth, a broken dream—in flesh and blood—and women screamed and grown men moaned. The ink was barely dry on the contract. The manager's wife discovered him and screamed. Ambulances and police cars clanged through the neighborhood, alerting the early risers and rousing sleepers. Neighbors poured out of brownstones and stood in tenement building windows, half-dressed, peering this way and that. Later, the manager's wife identified his body for the coroner's records.

Above the startled public was that window, opened ominously onto the street. A tall dark man in a turtleneck sweater, pipe hanging masterfully from his lip, casually addressed several onlookers. Each word of his assessment was loaded with tragic irony. "Whenever he was happy, he used to stand in that window—there—and shout his joy to the world."

The man moved on quietly. But several of the onlookers had heard and reported his statement to police officers. After a brief search of Dunny's twelfth floor apartment, it became official and the report of an accidental death was subsequently filed.

Between heaven and earth, the moments that mattered had flashed through Dunny's mind.

"Creative bookkeeping? What's that? Ricky, what's goin' on here, man. I ask you how come I'm almost broke when *Godlight* went platinum. And that's all you can say—which mean's nuthin' in my vocabulary."

"I'm sorry, Dunny. It's in your contract. They deduct all their expenses. And you're one-hundred percent responsible for taxes. It could take months before there's any profit on your side of the line. In the meantime, they'll advance you something on your next creative property."

"You shuckin' me."

"No. I'm not."

"And then the same thing just might happen again. I'm charged for studio time at who knows how much for an hour, the engineering costs, the recording costs. What! And I bet I pay for distribution as well. Who else is inflatin' the payroll? How many cousins, uncles, and flunkies?"

"Hey—hey, cool down, Dunny. You've gotta watch what you're sayin'."

"I didn't read the fine print because that's what I pay you for! I trusted you!"

"I did the best I could do for you, Dunny. You wanted on board. Don't forget, you were willing to compromise on the deal at the time."

"Like I knew what that meant. Like you told me."

"Did you really want to know?"

"I think I need to see an attorney."

"You can't afford one. And what makes you think they can't buy him out from under you?"

"Ricky—man, what am I supposed to do for more money? I thought I had it made. I bought a car, a house for my grandmother, and a new apartment uptown. I'm supposed to move in next week. Insurance up the ying-yang. How'm I gonna pay for all that, man?"

"Concentrate on your work. Keep workin' on your next album. I'll see what I can do."

"Do *something*, Ricky. Trade-offs, anything."

The sweetest gospel tenor in the history of the business, rolled those angelic notes heavenward, crossing easily into the popular culture and taking the attention of the industry by thunderstorm. No one had done the like since Mahalia Jackson. The media had been good to him. It was the answer to a childhood prayer. But he had not known that what was true for jazz and rock 'n' roll was also true for gospel. Had he known that all the bromides about fame were true, he would have taken a step back to prepare...

On odd mornings, the friendly signing of the contract was playing across his consciousness as he awakened. He found himself back at the Label, in the cloistered office of the president, listening to melodic strains of Debussy as they played under the façade of good will, polished mahogany, earth-toned leathers, and the odor of Cuban cigars. He could never see Ricky but could hear his voice and knew he was there. The alabaster bosses dressed in a casual elegance that seemed nearly Restoration in style, on the one hand, and devilish on the other.

"We're honest business men, Dunny."

"Plain, if not always simple."

"We have your interest at heart. But like everything else, there's a bottom line. When people like our product they buy. And the more they buy, the bigger your cut. You catch fire, Dunny, you catch fire! And here, right here! We'll renegotiate. Won't we? Won't you?"

"You damned straight, we will!"

He still could not see Ricky but felt his arm clasp his shoulders. It seemed a gesture of genuine affirmation.

"Understand the difference, Dunny. You have to appreciate the difference between hard people and bad people. We're not bad people. Not at all. But sometimes, we're hard."

* * *

Vellum found Dunny sitting glumly in the bar that night. He hated the taste of hard liquor, favoring sweet concoctions like piña coladas and tequila sunrises. He was focused on drinking himself into what he called "a stupor of sweetness."

"Dunny, don't do this." Vellum signaled to the waiter and had him remove the drinks. "Bring us some coffee—black."

"Go way, Vellum. Go away and leave me be."

"Stop it, Dunny. Stop being a child and grow up."

"I love you to death, Vellum. You're a great singer. But I don't want to do another album with you. I want to do my own thing. Otherwise, why bother?"

"Dunny—I understand."

"I'm a risin' star. You're a fallin' star. It ain't right and you know it ain't right. I'm sorry. I'm hurtin' your feelings. Me and my big mouth."

"Dunny—it wasn't my idea. None of it. I feel the same way you do. But I'm scared, Dunny. What will I do if I can't keep workin'? Who's gonna send my kids to college? What am I gonna live off of? I haven't had a solo hit make the charts above twenty-five in two years. But you and I, together, we were number one for six months! Think of it—six months!"

"Do dog food commercials. I want out of the deal. I want to do my own material, my way. *Godlight* was only the start. And it's charted five times, from number five to ten. Vellum—I've got so much more in me to give."

"Sure you do, Dunny. Sure you do. But go along with the Label on this one. Be smart, be patient. You'll get your chance."

"I had Ricky tell 'em I'd do anything. . . ." he blubbered, laying his head in the nest of her arms.

"And I'm your anything," she said in awe and wonder.

There were whispers in corridors and behind his back at parties. He felt the eyes, but when he turned no one was looking. Someone followed him everywhere, yet he never saw them. Guardian or spook? Every now and then, a notebook he scrawled lyrics in while at the office disappeared and was mysteriously returned to the same spot.

He began to talk loudly, to broadcast things that were harmful, things that could not be apologized for or retracted.

* * *

"Do you know that the mobsters own me?"

"I'm sorry, Dunny—I didn't quite get that."

"I said, do you know that I'm owned by mobsters."

"Oh. Are you?"

"You damned straight. Lock, stock, and barrel."

"Is that such a terrible thing?"

"Are you jivin'?"

"Well, that's a heavy rap. Do you have any solid evidence for this?"

"No—not hardly. But it's true."

"Um—Dunny, I'm just a music magazine writer, not an investigative reporter."

"Whatever that means."

"It means I'm here to interview you about your music. What new ideas you've come up with, what your ambitions are for the future—that sort of thing. The easy stuff your fans want to read about. To be honest—the fluff."

"My fans would puke if they knew how much shit I had to eat just for the privilege of walking into a recording studio. They'd puke if they knew I was in debt up to my eyeballs. If they knew the millions I purportedly make ain't mine to spend."

"Look—uh—Dunny, this is obviously a bad time for you. Why don't we reschedule. Say in a couple of days-when you've had some time."

"You're scared shitless. Just like the rest of 'em. I'm scared too. But I'm wearier of being scared than I am scared. How in the world am I supposed to be creative when I can't even think straight for being scared. I don't know how the others do it. Lord help me—and I do not take his name in vain—I don't know how."

"I'm sorry, Dunny. I've got to run. It's been a pleasure. Truly, it has. I'll be giving your secretary a call."

* * *

The crackup was a casual thing. He looked into the mirror and saw two heads staring back. He sat on the edge of the bathtub and closed his eyes. When he opened them again, he was sitting up in bed. How did he get there?

"It's not that uncommon an expression, Dunny. When one is divided against oneself."

"I'm afraid, Dr. Porter."

"I can give you something to help you sleep."

"What I need's an answer."

"What is the question? "

"Why do I feel so invisible when everybody knows who I am?"

That morning he rose with a song playing itself across his consciousness. He was drunk off fruitless thoughts, indecipherable nightmares, and the weight of disappointment. He had been refusing to open the door for anyone. Word had gotten around. Insofar as he was concerned, he called it "moling in," getting the rest everyone said he needed. Nevertheless, he started with the ritual shower, dressing in his own version of casual elegance, then breakfasted on hardtack and clabber, reminders of the backwoods roots from which he'd sprung.

His pauper's meal was interrupted by the heaviness of leather against the stone outside. A pounding on the door was followed by the plaintive voice of Ricky, nearly a cry. "Hey–Dunny, open up!"

He answered the door. Ricky's honey-toned countenance was pale yellow. He squirmed uneasily, backed away, turned, and ran. His absence was filled with a massive stony-eyed blackness that blocked all exits and stymied thought. The presence itself embodied the threat.

"Who–what–are you?"

He was greeted with an expressionless stare. Overcome by the recognition of danger, he turned to run for the exit off the kitchen. Unexpectedly, he was lifted off his feet, as if a bird or a cat, and hoisted through the air.

"Our faaaaathaaa who aaartt in he–ev–vaannn," Dunny sang as the sky parted, he plunged earthward and was received.

* * *

Vellum hurried to the site as soon as she heard. She frowned as her eyes measured the distance he had fallen. Had he lapsed into one of those hallucinations and scared himself into jumping? Had it been a simple misstep? An accident? Had something evil taken hold of him? A spokesman for the Label let it be known that Dunny was undergoing psychiatric care. The sun was setting. She knelt on the bloodied pavement and cried. Onlookers gathered. A child offered flowers and she placed them over the stain. Some recognized the famous soul singer, touched her gently with tentative fingers to acknowledge her sorrow. Then a long black limousine parted the crowd. A door opened and Vellum was escorted inside. It drove swiftly away. But the vigil continued. Reporters took photographs and talked to witnesses. Someone brought candles and lit them as others assembled, whispering his name, some holding hands softly saying prayers. Time passed and more and more the legend makers gathered as night deepened.

"Dunny," they chanted and whispered.

"Dunny, the dream is over, the song lives on."

143

Hibernation

It is always simmering under the palms, always hot. Heat rises from cement like sex from between thighs.

She loves this lusty southwestern climate.

Hers, a tropical zone of two seasons, summer and fall. When it rains, it is as if the earth has developed a fever and a severe sweat. Once in awhile it shudders and quakes, spilling fear onto the hearts of those who thought they would live forever. It is never long before the sun returns, a mad blaze of forced gaiety. Never long before beaches, patios, bistros, parks, and streets brim with thrillseekers, money-makers, and sightseers in various stages of yearning and undress.

Tragedy never takes hold here. It is a climate that breeds *bacillus frivolous.*

Outside she hears the muted din of ever-squirreling traffic. Chirps of starlings and barks of dogs pepper the air then fade. There is the continuous distant zoom of planes overhead. It is seldom long before violence stains the air, the asphalt, and the assonance. It may burst and break away, an old skin shed to reveal the new shine underneath. It may consume and distort, leaving a thick-crusted never-healing ulceration. It may relieve and release, the bowels in a tremulous swirl.

144

Once in awhile her ears prickle with shatters and bangs—a beer bottle, the window of a parked car, the collision of vehicles at an intersection nearby—all defining the parameters of fragile urban existence. Human conflict may lace the terrain like a contagion, yet it never disrupts the illusion fostered by the local lingo of facile reassurance: to be safe and secure, away from and above it all.

It is all as predictable as sunrise.

Post ravaging comes a shocked lull in which a scabbing over takes place. The charred soul is replanted, like burned topsoil dotted with mustard weed that smiles its yellow at the new sky. Fake smiles likewise erupt persistently against the psyche, eroding urgency, muting those stubborn clingers-on to despair and desperation.

What are you trying to capture?

Your pain.

Can you see it?

As you reveal it to me. Certainly.

And what does it look like, to you?

Something glorious.

How can pain be glorious?

It is the epitome of living. When living things experience pain, it brings their life force to the fore. The skin turns radiant. All that is strongest, worthy, and most beautiful rises to the surface and trembles before the eye. And it may be rendered by the seer in a work of art.

Quickly every troubled thing is healed over. A cosmic and cosmetic wonder. A milkwhite balm is applied, and scars vanish, revealing the beauty desired, but a dead cold beauty as consumptive as the violence.

She is in this and of it. Yet playing solo in summer is difficult and playing solo in fall, a terror.

How many seasons on her own?

The climate matures. For days at a time white mist may drift in off the Pacific, occlude skyscrapers and threaten flights. At times the air is frisky, blows clear, hard, and blue, reveals legs and betrays hairpieces. The heat and dry winds return. Pollen is everywhere. New growth overripens prematurely. Some ailing things are uprooted and die on their way to recovery. Evergreens and birds of paradise abound, as do broad well-shaded avenues and sun-washed homes. At brief times a darkening appears with, perhaps, the atmospheric specters of monsoons, which may flood streets and aspirations alike. Then the heat and winds swiftly return. Usually, the uncannily poised and lightly breezy heat prevails, a calm settles over the basin and deepens if the sunset cools.

What is spring?

Money and love go further in the fall. More places to go. Entertainment is rife. Children return to school. Introspection takes on depth and weight.

Sunday nights and Sunday mornings are the dreaded. Friends are with family, or stay in for a last respite before the return to work. Thoughts and fears become roomsize, shadows take on substance, rattle locked doors, comb the refrigerator for treats, climb into the pillows. Cry and rage at the crying.

Why are there no takers for what she offers?

Why didn't things work out?

Will things ever work out?

How many options does she have? What choices?

Who will care enough?

Who will make her his?

Does he exist? Where is he? What is he? If she does find him, what can he, will he, do?

These questions go unanswered even in sleep. The stereo left on, a lullaby around the clock, a parade of rhythms and blues to drown out the absence of telephone rings. The television left on also, a tireless network illuminating the silence, the flow of outmoded movie dialogue and used car jingles underscoring each dreamscape.

The dreams themselves are willed into a sameness. His arms will be the holding kind. His eyes will be caverns of warmth and understanding. However tall, he will be the perfect height. However he looks, he will be handsome. Whatever his flaws, he will be perfect. Whatever the struggle, she will find happiness.

His love, she imagines, will take her into another realm, arouse an unspeakable glory in shocking ripples. His scent, his heat—breath so suddenly shared. In the climate of his smile she will become delirious

146

with giving, their world a sanctuary in a spectrum of blue, endless bright blue waves of enchantment, so dutifully joyously blue.

In the workday dawn, the inhabited dream bursts, the rooms fill with an intrusive yellowness, the cracks of reality revealed. She rises as always, begins her morning ritual.

In the bathroom she runs hot water into the tub, perfumes it.

She sets out creams, potions, soaps. Undressing, she seeks herself in the mirror. She stares at, then into, her reflection, teases the doubts. She scrubs out those subterranean chambers, down to the everlasting echoes—wonders at her beauty, the delicious goodness, the impish playfulness, the spirited laughter, the heady heavy sweetness, and sees the girl, the woman, the crone, all her selves present in the moment.

She slips into the tub and allows the heat its soothing soak. She reminds herself: this state of stillness is only temporary, a hibernation. Her season will come and suspension end. All she need do is maintain. So there. Her only choice is made. Until he makes her his. Until then, she waits. Like the city, always simmering, heat rising from the sumptuous asphalt of her skin. Ever waiting to be borne on that balmy promised crescendo.

Sources and Acknowledgments

The first epigraph is from the poem "Solitudes Crowded with Loneliness," by Robert Kaufman, from *Solitudes Crowded with Loneliness*, copyright © 1965 by Bob Kaufman. Reprinted by permission of New Directions Publishing Corp. and Coffee House Press.

The second epigraph is the poem "Tarpaulin," from *Self-Portrait in a Convex Mirror* by John Ashbery, copyright © 1972, 1973, 1974, 1975 by John Ashbery. Used by permission of Viking Penguin, a division of Penguin Group (USA) Inc.

"Lush Life," Words and Music by Billy Strayhorn. Copyright © 1949; Renewed 1977 Dimensional Music Of 1091 (ASCAP) and Billy Strayhorn Songs, Inc. (ASCAP) Rights for Dimensional Music Of 1091 and Billy Strayhorn Songs, Inc. Administered by Cherry Lane Music Publishing Company, Inc. International Copyright Secured. All Rights Reserved.

"Butterfly Meat" appeared in *Michigan Quarterly Review*, Vol. 39, No. 3 (Ann Arbor: University of Michigan, 2000).

"Pepper" appeared in excerpted form in the *Los Angeles Times Book Review*, April 16, 2000. An expanded version appeared in *Obsidian* III, Vol. 2, No. 1 (Raleigh: Department of English, North Carolina State University, 2000).

"Jazz at Twelve" appeared in *Brilliant Corners: A Journal of Jazz & Literature*, Vol. 5, No. 2 (Williamsport: Lycoming College, 2001).

"Backcity Transit by Day" appeared in *High Plains Literary Review*, Vol. XVI, Nos. 2 and 3 (Denver: Fall/Winter 2001). It was reprinted in *Griots Beneath the Baobab: Tales from Los Angeles*, edited by Randy Ross and Erin Aubry Kaplan (Los Angeles: International Black Writers & Artists of Los Angeles, 2002).

"Purgatory" appeared in *TRIBES: A Gathering of Tribes Multicultural Magazine* (New York: Spring/Summer 1993).

"My Brain's Too Tired To Think" appeared in *ZYZZYVA: The Last Word: West Coast Writers & Artists*, Vol. XVIII, No. 2 (San Francisco: 2001).

"Shark Liver Oil" appeared in *Gargoyle*, No. 44 (Arlington: 2002).

"Darkness" appeared in *Long Shot*, Vol. 24 (Hoboken: Long Shot Publications, 2000).

The remaining stories—"Joy Ride," "Winona's Choice," "My Son, My Son," "Dunny," and "Hibernation"—appear here for the first time.

WANDA COLEMAN was born in Watts in 1946 and raised in the Los Angeles community of South Central. To support herself as a writer, she has worked as a medical secretary, magazine editor, journalist, and scriptwriter, occasionally moonlighting as a waitress or bartender. In 1971 she began her thirty-year association with Black Sparrow Press (now Black Sparrow Books, an imprint of David R. Godine, Publisher), during which she published sixteen books of poetry and prose, beginning with a chapbook of poems in 1977. She has received literary fellowships from the National Endowment for the Arts and the Guggenheim Foundation for poetry. Her honors in fiction include a fellowship from the California Arts Council and the 1990 Harriet Simpson Arnow Prize from *The American Voice*. She received the 1999 Lenore Marshall Poetry Prize for *Bathwater Wine* from the Academy of American Poets, *The Nation*, and the New Hope Foundation. Her collection *Mercurochrome: New Poems* was a bronze-medal finalist for the 2001 National Book Awards in Poetry and a finalist for the 2002 Paterson Poetry Prize. An electrifying presenter of her work, famed for her readings (Bumbershoot Festival, Berlin Literary Festival, Manhattan Theatre Club, Shakespeare & Company), she has become known as "the L.A. Blueswoman." In 2003 she became the first literary artist to receive a C.O.L.A. Fellowship from the Los Angeles Department of Cultural Affairs. She resides in Southern California with her husband Austin Straus and family.